You're in Control

CREEPOVER

Don't Drink the Punch!

written by P. J. N

SIMON SPOTLIGHT

New York London Toronto Sydney New Delhi

This book is a work of fiction. Any references to historical events, real people, or real places are used fictitiously. Other names, characters, places, and events are products of the author's imagination, and any resemblance to actual events or places or persons, living or dead, is entirely coincidental.

SIMON SPOTLIGHT
An imprint of Simon & Schuster Children's Publishing Division
1230 Avenue of the Americas, New York, New York 10020
Copyright © 2012 by Simon & Schuster, Inc.
Text by Sarah Albee
Designed by Nicholas Sciacca
All rights reserved, including the right of reproduction in whole or in part in any form.
SIMON SPOTLIGHT and colophon are registered trademarks of Simon & Schuster, Inc.
YOU'RE INVITED TO A CREEPOVER is a trademark of Simon & Schuster, Inc.
For information about special discounts for bulk purchases, please contact Simon & Schuster Special Sales at 1-866-506-1949 or business@simonandschuster.com.
Manufactured in the United States of America 0313 OFF
First Edition 10 9 8 7 6 5 4 3
ISBN 978-1-4424-5287-9
ISBN 978-1-4424-5288-6 (eBook)
Library of Congress Catalog Card Number 2012934010

PROLOGUE

Mr. Talbert yawned as he tried to hold a stack of uncorrected lab papers and his coffee cup in one hand and unlock his classroom door with the other. Feeble early-morning light filtered through the high windows and reflected off the surfaces of the lab tables. He flicked on the overhead, flooding the room with harsh fluorescent light. He yawned again as he headed for his desk, wondering if he'd have time this Friday morning to finish grading all the labs before first period.

He plopped the stack of papers down on his desk. Then he scratched his head quizzically and regarded the life-size skeleton next to his desk. The skeleton's head was cocked at a jaunty angle. It stared back at him with its shadowy, unseeing eyes.

"Did I just see what I think I saw?" he asked the skeleton.

The skeleton didn't answer.

Mr. Talbert took three backward steps. He turned toward the bug terrarium that sat on the counter running the length of his classroom. The counter was cluttered with mineral samples, animal skulls, and fossils.

The lid of the terrarium was askew. He crouched down to peer into it.

The day before it had contained a bustling little ecosystem, filled with at least a dozen large green scarab beetles, scientific name *Chelorrhina polyphemus*, crawling around on the sandy bottom and gnawing on the bits of apple his middle school students had dropped in. But now the terrarium was empty. The beetles were nowhere to be seen.

Mr. Talbert turned back to the skeleton. "They can't have climbed out on their own," he said. "Someone's taken them!"

The skeleton didn't answer.

CHAPTER 1

"Um, Jess? No offense, but that hat?" Alice mock-shuddered. "So last year."

Jess reached up and touched her hat, smiling ruefully at Alice. "I know, I know. But it was so cold this morning when I ran out of the house, and I left my good one in my locker at school."

"I always buy two of everything," pronounced Pria. "That way I have a spare."

Kayla, who was picking her way along the icy sidewalk a step behind the other three girls, furrowed her brow. She *liked* Jess's hat. It was a dusty rose color with a folded-up brim that set off Jess's delicate features and wide-set green eyes. But Kayla would never dream of piping up and disagreeing with Alice. No one wanted to invite Alice's criticism if they could help it. Kayla wondered if Pria was serious about buying two of everything. Like *that* would ever happen in Kayla's house. She glanced down at her winter boots, which were very definitely so *two* years ago. Her mom had found them last year at an end-of-season clearance sale, and Kayla had been delighted with them.

"Brrrr!" said Jess, hunkering deeper into her luxurious down coat. "It must be negative a hundred degrees today. Probably a record low for Fairbridge, Minnesota."

"Even Buttercup looks like he feels cold, which is a miracle considering all the natural insulation that dog has," said Alice, gesturing to the dog at the end of the rhinestone-studded leash she was holding in her gloved hand. "My mom says she's going to put him on a diet."

"It's the wind," said Kayla. "That's what makes it feel so cold."

As if to emphasize Kayla's point, an icy gust of crystallized snow sprang up and swirled around the girls. All four put their heads down to shield their faces against the needlelike blast. Kayla could feel the icy snow blowing down the back of her coat collar and up her coat sleeves, which were getting a little too short for her.

"Buttercup! Slow *down*, you dumb dog!" said Alice, lunging forward from the force of the dog's tugging. Buttercup kept straining at his leash.

Kayla usually liked dogs, but Buttercup had to be the ugliest dog she'd ever seen, and he was not especially friendly, either. His snout was all pushed in, as though he had run face-first into a glass patio door. His tail curled up and around backward, so that it practically formed a circle. He didn't walk so much as he waddled, his round belly shifting from side to side. Alice had told her that he was a very rare and valuable breed. Whatever.

Pria adjusted her fuzzy pink earmuffs. "Please tell me why we're out here again?"

"I'm behaving like the model citizen," said Alice with a half smile. "I've offered to walk Buttercup every single afternoon so my parents will stick to their promise to let me have the party."

"It's so awesome that you're going to have a coed Valentine's party," said Pria.

"Yeah, I'm psyched. The girls get to sleep over, and the boys will all leave at eleven," said Alice.

"Will you guys help me find a cute party outfit at the mall today?" asked Jess.

"I'm going to buy at least three outfits," said Alice, ignoring Jess's question. "Then I'll be able to choose whatever I'm in the mood for on the day of the party."

"Speaking of shopping," said Pria, "have you *noticed* the stores on this block? I mean, who shops here? Especially considering there's a perfectly good mall nearby."

"Clearly no one, from the looks of these places," said Alice with a sniff.

Kayla clutched the collar of her coat and looked up, squinting as another blast of icy wind sprang up.

It was true. For a generally swanky town like theirs, this seemed to be the one-block-long low-rent district. It was doubly strange that such a run-down block existed in this part of town, of all places, because Alice lived just four blocks away, on one of the fanciest streets in Fairbridge.

They passed an antique store, with a dimly lit storefront displaying a jumble of threadbare old armchairs that looked like they'd seen much better days. Next door was a discount clothing store called Dressed Best, displaying mannequins with no heads or hands, modeling unfashionable dresses. And just past that was a shop with a sign reading ESOTERICA: SPIRITUAL SUPPLIES · CANDLES · OILS · SPELLS. The snow on the sidewalk seemed undisturbed in front of the shops, as though no one had gone in or out in some time.

"Buttercup! I told you to stop *pulling*, you awful little thing," said Alice. "After thousands of dollars of obedience training, he's still the most annoying dog!" She lurched as Buttercup bounded forward, barking his head off at something the girls couldn't see, something behind the recessed door of the dress shop.

"It's a cat," said Pria.

Just then Buttercup managed to slip out of his collar, leaving Alice holding the empty leash. He moved much more quickly on his short legs than Kayla would have thought he could, dashing toward the doorway and yapping furiously.

A black cat streaked across the sidewalk, heading toward the road. Kayla watched, stricken, as it leaped over the mound of plowed, grayish snow and into the road, just as an oncoming car was passing. The cat landed right in front of the car, and the girls couldn't see whether one of the car's tires rolled over it. The driver, a man talking on his cell phone, kept going, apparently unaware of what had happened.

Buttercup struggled to mount the ploughed snow-bank, still in pursuit of the cat, and Alice was able to grab him and snap his collar back on. Then she peered over the edge of the snowbank at the place where the cat had fallen.

"Is it dead?" Jess called to Alice in a small voice.

"Maybe," Alice replied grimly.

The other three girls moved closer to look, peering fearfully over the snowbank.

The cat lay unmoving in a pile of slush.

"Let's get out of here," said Alice. "I so don't need to deal with this right now."

"But what about the cat?" asked Kayla, staring down at it in horror.

"It was probably just a stray," said Jess. "I agree. Let's go."

"It's wearing a collar," Kayla pointed out.

"Come *on*," said Alice. "My mom said she'd take us to the mall as soon as we got back, and it's *freezing* out here."

The other two girls turned to follow Alice. Kayla stood there. "I'm going to check on the cat," she said. "I'll catch up to you in a minute."

Alice scowled. "Whatever. But hurry up. I can't guarantee that my mom will wait very long."

Kayla watched the other three girls hurry away through the swirling, misting snow. After making sure no cars were coming, she stepped gingerly over the snowbank and looked down at the cat. Its body lay stretched out, its head facing her, its limbs sprawled in an awkward, uncatlike way.

She was afraid to touch it. Was it breathing, or was that just the wind stirring its fur? She crouched down. "Sorry, kitty," she whispered. "I'm sorry about that dumb dog."

She saw no blood, thank goodness, but then, it would be awfully hard to see blood on a coal-black cat like this one. She grew more certain that it was dead. She looked up at the row of stores. Was anyone looking out the window? Even if they were, they wouldn't be able to see the cat's body, which would be hidden by the bank of snow. She saw no one. She stared back down at the cat.

"I wonder what your name was," she said sadly. And then, as if to answer her, its eyes flew open.

CHAPTER 2

Kayla jumped up. "Oh!" she gasped. "You're alive!"

The cat fumbled against the snowbank and tried to sit up.

"I need to get you out of the street," said Kayla. Luckily, it was a quiet street. Not a single car had passed since the one that had knocked down the cat.

The cat managed to sit up. It shook its head rapidly back and forth, as though trying to shake out the cobwebs.

"Can you walk, kitty?" asked Kayla.

As though it had understood, the cat rose shakily onto its feet. It took a tentative step and collapsed nose-down in the snow. It let out a low growl.

"It's your front leg, isn't it?" guessed Kayla.

The cat sat down on its haunches and blinked at Kayla. It raised its right front paw into the air, almost like a dog might offer its paw to shake.

Kayla glanced up again at the shops. No one was emerging. She looked across the street. Practically the whole block was taken up by a restaurant supply store, but it had a sign that said CLOSED: LOST OUR LEASE on the door.

"Will you let me carry you?" she asked the cat. She took a step toward it and reached gently underneath it to pick it up. It let out a longer, more ominous growl, but it allowed her to do so. She was careful not to touch its front leg.

It was a large, heavy cat. Kayla held it close to her chest and turned to clamber back over the snowdrift, hoping she wouldn't slip. Her boot sank deeply into the snow, and a chunk of ice slipped into the back of it.

"Let's try the antique store," she said to the cat, and made her way carefully over to the doorway of the first shop. Crouching awkwardly, she managed to turn the rickety knob without dropping the cat. She pushed the door, hearing a little bell tinkle.

The inside of the store smelled musty, like old leather boots, but at least it was warm. The shelves were crammed with old bottles and dusty china figurines, and a display case in the middle held cheap costume jewelry. The wares looked more like they should be at a flea market than at an antique store, Kayla thought.

"Help you?" said someone in the back. A large woman emerged from around the back counter, regarding Kayla suspiciously. "We don't allow pets in here," she said, eyeing the cat over the tops of her glasses.

"Um, hi," said Kayla. "This isn't my pet. I saw this cat get hit by a car, and I wondered if you might know who it belongs to. It's not dead or anything, but I think its paw is hurt."

The woman looked again at the cat in Kayla's arms. "Not mine," she said with a shrug. "And not Betty's next door. She's always complaining about her allergies."

Kayla drooped. "Well, thanks anyway," she said, and turned to leave.

"You might try two doors down at that hocus-pocus shop. I never have laid eyes on the owner—he's certainly not a friendly chap—but I seem to recall seeing a cat wandering around outside the store from time to time."

Kayla nodded. "Okay, thanks," she said, and opening the chiming door, she stepped back outside into the swirling cold.

The cat was not a cuddly sort of cat. It allowed her to carry it down the short block, but it felt like a dead weight in her arms. They were beginning to ache with holding it.

"I hope this is your owner," said Kayla as she opened the door to the mystical store. "I need to get back to Alice's house."

This shop smelled like cinnamon and musky perfume and something Kayla couldn't identify—a faint, acrid smell that reminded her of the time she'd accidentally set a tendril of her hair on fire when she was blowing out her birthday candles.

"Hello?" she called out. "Anyone here?"

She looked around. What kind of store *was* this, anyway? The walls were painted a deep red, so despite the overhead light, the place looked dark and shadowy. A bloodred velvet curtain hung in the doorway to the back, near the register. The walls were lined with shelves from floor to ceiling, and the shelves held neat rows of bottles, each labeled by hand in the same swirly cursive writing. Kayla couldn't make out what any of the labels said from where she was standing. There was one of those sliding wooden ladders she'd seen in old movies, the kind that could move on a rail so the shop owner could reach things up high. Along the back wall were hand-lettered signs: SPELL CANDLES: LIGHT ONE TO MANIFEST YOUR INTENTIONS AND DESIRES; HEALING CRYSTALS: HANDPICKED FOR THEIR BEAUTY AND HEALING ENERGY; ELIXIRS: POTIONS INFUSED WITH HERBAL ESSENCES; MAGICAL OILS: AROMATHERAPY OIL BLENDS TO SUPPORT TRANSFORMATION.

Kayla was stooping down to read the label on a bottle (LOVE POTION: WIN THE PASSION OF THAT SPECIAL SOMEONE!) when she heard footsteps. She stood up hastily, shifting the cat a bit in her arms. The cat growled in protest.

A girl stood at the other end of the store, regarding her. "May I help you?" she said. "Hey, what are you doing with Jinx?"

"Oh! So this is your cat?" asked Kayla. "He got knocked down. By a car. I think he's okay, but his front leg is hurt."

The girl frowned and strode across the store. She took the cat from Kayla's arms. Kayla took a small step back and blinked at her.

The girl was about Kayla's age, although a good six inches shorter. She seemed familiar. Wasn't she in Kayla's grade at school? They weren't in any classes together, but

Kayla was sure she'd seen her around. Was it Madeline? Melinda? She wore huge, owlish glasses. Her straight, bluntly cut bangs hid a good part of her face.

"Jinx never goes into the street. Something must have spooked him. What happened?" the girl asked Kayla. She looked up accusingly, her bangs parting like a curtain and revealing a nose that was somewhat too large for her thin face.

"Nothing. I mean, I don't know," Kayla stammered. "He ran into the road and bumped into the side of a car that was passing by."

The girl snorted, then carried Jinx over to a glass display table that housed some sparkly stones. She set the cat gently down on the table. It immediately began licking its paw, slowly, as though assessing where it hurt.

"Do you work here?" asked Kayla, looking around.

"It's my after-school and weekend job," said the girl. Her tone was gruff and unfriendly. "The owner lets me work the register because I'm very responsible." She leaned over the cat, blowing her bangs away diagonally with the corner of her mouth so as to see more closely, and ran her hand down the animal's back, then down each paw, gently pressing as she went, as carefully as a trained veterinarian. "Looks like a simple radial fracture," she muttered, more to herself than to Kayla or the cat.

Suddenly she stood up and wheeled on Kayla.

"He didn't just run into the road, did he? Something scared him. Your dog, maybe?"

"No!" Kayla said quickly. "I mean, maybe. My friend's dog might have . . . might have startled him a little."

"Get out of here," the girl said in a low, ominous voice.

CHAPTER 3

Kayla backed away and turned to search for the door-knob. This girl freaked her out. She pulled the door open. Cold wind howled and swirled into the shop, setting several sets of chimes tinkling.

"Wait," the girl called. The tone of her voice was strained but suddenly friendly.

Kayla shut the door again and turned.

"What's your name?"

"Kayla Evans."

"I'm Matilda Warner. You go to Fairbridge Middle, don't you?"

Kayla nodded.

"And you're friends with that horrible Alice Grafton and her social-climbing friends, aren't you?"

"I—that's not very—"

"You moved here last year?"

Kayla nodded, wondering how Matilda knew so much about her. She wanted to get out of there. "From Texas."

"What does your mother do?"

Kayla was perplexed by Matilda's sudden interest in her. But she answered, "My mom got a job at Fairbridge Academy, in the admissions office, so we moved."

"Oh. No wonder those girls are your friends. No doubt they think your mother can help get them into the academy for high school," said Matilda.

Kayla felt like she'd been punched in the stomach. She had been trying so hard to make friends in this new town. She didn't want to think that they were just using her.

"What's your dad do?"

Kayla looked down. "He's dead."

Matilda grunted. "You have brothers and sisters?"

"Yes, three brothers. All younger."

Another grunt. "So why do you hang out with that clique of horrid rich girls?"

Kayla furrowed her brow. "Well, I, um . . ."

18

"Never mind, I can see you're just trying to fit in, find your way in that huge middle school. Well, take my advice. Alice Grafton is mean and vain and superficial, and her life revolves around being idolized. She's bad news. And so are her awful friends, Pria Patel and Jess Hunnicut. They follow her around like she's the queen of Sheba." Matilda sniffed. "Anyway, I suppose I should thank you for helping Jinx. He has a fracture, but the vet can fix it. He should be fine."

"You're welcome," said Kayla.

"You seem decent enough. Not like the others."

Kayla wasn't sure what to say. *Thank you? What?* But she just nodded and put her hand back on the knob. "I have to go now," she said to Matilda.

"Hey, why don't you bring your friends by the shop sometime?" suggested Matilda.

Kayla blinked. "I thought you said they were awful."

"I was just kidding. They're great. Bring them by. We have all kinds of elixirs and potions they might be interested in."

"Like what?" asked Kayla, very confused by Matilda's sudden change in mood. Clearly this Matilda was a strange girl, and Kayla knew she had to hurry to catch up with her friends before they left for the mall. But her curiosity got the better of her.

"All kinds. Beauty potions, complexion creams, love potions, essential oils that improve your mental processing. You seem pretty smart, but some of your flibbertigibbet friends could use a little help in that department," said Matilda.

"Um, sure, great, thanks," said Kayla, wondering what a flibbertigibbet was. "I'll tell them. I hope Jinx feels better soon."

As she left, she caught a glimpse of Matilda and Jinx through the glass door, staring at her. The light glinted off Matilda's huge glasses, so it was impossible to see her expression, and Jinx's eyes seemed to glow green. As she wrestled to close the door against the gusting wind, Kayla thought she heard something. It sounded like laughter.

She walked as fast as she dared along the icy sidewalk, but the light was fading and the wind kept blowing her coat open, making it hard to see her feet. Left at the corner, two blocks down, and another right, and she found herself back on Alice's block. It felt like it was a world away from the block she'd come from. The street was much wider, and houses on either side were set far back, with expansive lawns and large, overhanging trees. Alice's house was the biggest one on the block, red brick and three stories tall. Kayla had been there many times—in fact, the girls were sleeping over at Alice's tonight, and Kayla had left her overnight bag there when they went to walk Buttercup.

The lights were all on, but no one answered when she rang the bell. She rang again and waited. She heard Buttercup barking like crazy from inside, and listened for footsteps, but heard nothing. The front door was locked. She headed back down the front stoop and made her way around the side, to the kitchen door. When no one answered her knock, she tried the knob. It was unlocked. She stepped into the brightly lit kitchen. "Hello?" she called. "Anyone here?"

Except for Buttercup, who was now glaring at her from the doorway, growling from deep in his throat, the house was silent.

CHAPTER 4

Kayla looked around the huge kitchen. It was about three times the size of her mother's kitchen, and except for the fancy six-burner stove, the appliances were nearly invisible to the eye—the refrigerator and dish-washer were covered with the same wood paneling as the kitchen cupboards. A marble island dominated the center of the large room, and on it sat three mugs and a plate with two cookies on it. The chairs were pushed back, as though the people sitting in them had suddenly dashed off somewhere in the middle of a snack. She stomped her boots on the mat and then walked over to the saucepan that sat on the stove. She touched the side of the pot. It was still warm, and about a third full of cocoa.

Kayla furrowed her brow. She guessed Alice wasn't lying when she said her mother wouldn't wait. Then she saw a piece of pink paper under the table. It must have blown to the floor when she'd opened the door. She stooped down to pick it up. It was a note to her, written in Alice's lovely, girly handwriting. Kayla wished that her own handwriting was that pretty.

We waited for you, but my mom says we have to leave for the mall now. She has an exercise class to get to. Meet us there? The number for the taxi service is on the fridge. Text me when you get there.
A.

Kayla frowned. Why couldn't they have just texted her? They could probably have picked her up on her way from the strange shop to Alice's. Now she'd have to walk to the mall. There was no way she could afford to pay for a taxi service. She looked outside. It was dusk, a late February afternoon. It would probably be dark in about twenty more minutes. She could hear the pitter-patter of the blustering snow against the window.

"I'll call Mom," she said out loud. She pulled out her cell phone and hit the number to her mother's office.

"Hi, honey," her mother greeted her. But she pronounced the words "Hah, huney," with her Texan drawl. Kayla was convinced that not only had her mother not tried to lose her Southern accent, she'd purposely made it sound more pronounced since they'd moved to Minnesota. It was almost as though she was proud of it.

"Hi, Mom. Any chance you can swing by Alice's and give me a lift to the mall? They had to, um, leave without me."

She prayed her mother wouldn't make a big fuss about this. She knew her mother wasn't quite sure about Alice.

Her mother was quiet for a moment. "All right. I was just about to leave the office anyway. I'll be there in five minutes."

"Thanks, Mom," said Kayla, welling up with gratitude that her mother hadn't asked any questions. She had forgotten that her mother had gone into the office today—a Saturday. She probably was too distracted with all the work she was trying to get through to question why the others had left without her.

A short while later, Kayla was climbing into her mother's battered old minivan. The front passenger door was stuck, so she had to enter through the sliding side door and then push her way into the front seat. "You're great to do this," she said, as her mother pulled out of the driveway. "I hope this didn't make you leave work early."

Her mom shook her head and laughed ruefully. "I have a stack of applications to get through, and I can't get anything done at the office. Anyway, the babysitter wants to leave early tonight to go on a date with her new boyfriend, and Timothy has hockey practice at seven, so it's just as well I left the office when I did."

"Remember I told you about Alice's Valentine's Day party next Saturday?" Kayla said, as they pulled into the mall parking lot. "It's okay if I go, right?"

"It's coed, right?" asked her mother. "I need to call Alice's mother and confirm that adults will be there. But assuming there are chaperones, of course you can go, honey."

Kayla cringed inwardly. She felt ashamed to admit it to herself, but she dreaded the idea of her mother talking to Alice's mom. That accent, ugh. Maybe her mother would get just a tiny bout of laryngitis and have to e-mail Mrs. Grafton instead.

"I am positive there will be grown-ups there," said Kayla. "Maybe you can just e-mail her or something."

Her mother stopped at the curb in front of the main entrance. "We'll see, honey. Have fun with your friends. Don't stay up all night tonight."

Kayla opened the sliding door. She waved to her mom and hurried inside.

CHAPTER 5

"Kaylaaaa!" called Alice from across the food court. "Over here!"

Kayla spotted their table and hurried over, plopping herself wearily into a chair. Jess was sipping a frothy pink milkshake, and Alice and Pria had hot drinks piled with swirls of whipped cream.

"Sorry we had to leave without you," said Alice, who didn't sound very sorry at all. "My mom can be *so* annoying sometimes. She can't miss one second of her exercise class." She made a pouty face and blinked her long eyelashes at Kayla.

Kayla suspected this tactic of seeking forgiveness worked for Alice more often than not. The seventh-grade boys all seemed to be obsessed with her. It probably helped that she had beautiful, glossy hair with never a strand out of place, and her outfits always looked like they were designed by a professional stylist.

"It's okay," said Kayla. She glanced under the table at three large shopping bags. "What did you guys get?"

"There were so many cute things at Ozzie's," Pria gushed. "I bought three tops!"

Kayla smiled and nodded. She had never once set foot in Ozzie's, which always had music blasting from the speakers and huge black-and-white posters in the windows, showing bored-looking, ultracool teens lounging around in hundred-dollar shirts and expensively distressed jeans.

"Don't worry, though," said Alice, jumping to her feet. "We'll find something for you. We are so not done shopping, right?"

The other girls stood up and began collecting their cups and bags. Suddenly Alice sat back down.

"Don't look! Don't look!" she hissed, staring intently at the cup on the table in front of her.

Of course the girls looked.

"He's walking straight toward us. He's with Scott and Anthony. How do I look? I totally have hat hair. I know it."

The other girls sat back down too. "Stop, Alice. You look amazing," said Jess. "Nick Maroulis would be an idiot not to *beg* you to go out with him. That's probably what he's about to do right now."

Alice finger-combed her hair and then shook it out, so that it tumbled fetchingly around her face. "They're almost here. Don't look. Don't *look*. Just act normal. Oh, hey, guys!"

"Hey, what's up?" said Nick.

He certainly is good-looking, Kayla thought, admiring the way his jacket emphasized his broad shoulders and narrow waist. He was already pretty tall, and he towered over most of the other seventh-grade boys. But Kayla didn't really like him or trust him. Maybe it was the fact that he was always rude to their teachers in class, or that he cared more about his hair than being nice to his classmates.

"We're just hanging out," said Alice, sounding oh so casual.

"I got into way too much trouble at Ozzie's," Pria said to Scott Mallory with a giggle. "My dad is going to be mad when he gets the bill."

Scott's mouth turned up in a little smile, but Kayla

could see that he was not a bit interested in stories about shopping.

"Yeah, so, we were thinking about going to a movie in a little while," said Alice. "That new horror flick that got such good reviews? It's playing right upstairs at the Cineplex."

This was news to Kayla. She mentally tallied up how much money she had with her. Maybe if she didn't get any popcorn or soda, she could swing a ticket.

Nick looked at Scott and Anthony, who both shrugged noncommittally. "Yeah, sorry, we're supposed to go to the basketball game over at Fairbridge Academy," said Nick. "My older brother's playing against them, and it's the semifinals."

"No biggie," said Alice, stretching back in her chair and extending her long, lovely legs out in front of her. "All the more popcorn for us!"

Jess and Pria giggled. Kayla remembered now. Pria liked Scott, and Jess liked Anthony Schmidt. No wonder they were giggling like silly hyenas.

"Hey, have you guys seen my cousin around?" asked Scott.

Kayla's heart thumped inside her chest. Was he talking about Tom?

The girls shook their heads.

"He is such a dork sometimes," said Scott, shaking his head. "He said he wanted to check out some book at the bookstore and, like, ditched us."

Pria giggled like that was the funniest thing anyone had ever said.

Kayla was now sitting forward, perking up her ears. She had had a secret crush on Tom Butler for months now, but hadn't dared mention it to her friends. For one thing, he was at least two inches shorter than she was, although his feet were gigantic. He cheerfully referred to himself as a human L. She liked his self-deprecating humor, his goofy sideways grin, and his spot-on impersonations of all the seventh-grade teachers and school administrators. But Alice had made several disparaging comments about him, and he was obviously not part of the cool crowd.

"Hey, do you think it was your cousin Tom who let those bugs go in Talbert's classroom yesterday?" asked Anthony.

Scott shrugged. "I doubt it. He's not really the practical joker kind of dude. I could see him taking one out and studying it under a microscope, but I don't think he'd just have let them go."

"Well, whoever did it should be arrested," said Alice. "Those disgusting bugs. They could be anywhere now. One of them could crawl inside my *locker* or something!" She shuddered. "But I guess I should invite your cousin to my party, huh," Alice said to Scott.

"That would be good," said Scott. "Avoid a little awkwardness with my mom and aunt."

"When is it again?" asked Nick.

Alice slumped, exasperation written across her face. "Hel-lo? Next *Saturday*? Which is, in case you forgot, *Valentine's* Day?"

Nick grinned sheepishly. "Oh yeah."

Anthony checked his phone. "That's my dad," he said. "We better roll if we want to make it for the tip-off."

"I'll tell Tom to meet us in front," said Scott, pulling out his own phone.

"See you," said Nick, loping away. The other boys followed.

As soon as they'd been swallowed up in the crowds of shoppers, Alice sighed deeply and slumped down in her chair. "He just doesn't seem all that into me," she said, looking puzzled. "I mean, okay, I guess I see why Scott and Anthony haven't made up their minds about liking you two"—she waved a hand in the direction of Jess and Pria—"but why is it that all the guys in school worship me except the one guy I have a crush on?"

Kayla started to laugh, thinking Alice was joking, and then realized she wasn't. How could Alice say such things to Pria and Jess without their getting mad at her? And how amazing it must be to have so much self-confidence.

"Are we really going to the movie?" asked Jess, pretending that Alice hadn't just insulted her.

"No, I just floated that in case they said they'd come with us," said Alice. She stood up. "Let's go do some more shopping."

Kayla followed the girls from store to store for the next two hours as they tried on outfit after outfit, accumulating mounds of shopping bags.

"Aren't you going to try anything on?" asked Alice as she appeared outside the dressing room. She was trying on a close-fitting red dress with a fluttery hemline, and she looked amazing as she turned this way and that, gazing at her reflection in the three-way mirror.

"Nah, don't think so," said Kayla. "I think I already found just the right outfit for the party." But this was a lie. She was thinking about asking her mother to take her to that discount clothing store, the one next to that odd mystical shop. *Maybe I'll find something to wear there,* she thought doubtfully.

Back at Alice's later that night, the girls finished watching a movie in Alice's spacious bedroom. Then they arranged their sleeping bags in a circle, so they could have their heads together and be able to talk late into the night.

"I'm so bummed about Nick," Alice said with a sigh.

"Yeah, me too," said Pria. "I mean, I'm bummed too, but about Scott," she added quickly. "He doesn't seem all that into *me,* either."

"Anthony barely even says hi to me in the halls," said Jess. She sighed glumly and reached for a handful of chips.

"Do *you* like anyone?" Alice asked Kayla.

"Me? No. No one," said Kayla quickly.

Alice's eyes narrowed. "You so like someone," she said. "Will you tell us if we guess? I bet I know. It's Scott's cousin Tom, isn't it? Say it isn't, Kay. He is *such* a nerd!"

Kayla blushed. "I so do not like Tom," she said unconvincingly.

"You so do," replied Alice. "We need to find someone better for you to like. I can't have one of my friends liking a dork like Tom."

"No, really, I—" Kayla needed to think of a way to change the subject, fast. "Hey, you guys remember that cat that almost got run over?"

"Oh yeah!" said Jess. "Was it dead? Did you find out who owned it?"

Kayla described the events of the afternoon, and how she'd discovered that Jinx belonged to the owner of the mystical shop. Then she told them about the strange girl, Matilda.

"I totally know that girl," said Alice, scrambling to a sitting position. "She moved here a year before you did, Kay. We were in the same fifth grade together. She is super weird."

"She's emo," added Jess.

Alice glared at her, displeased at being interrupted. Then she continued, "Back in fifth grade, she was huge, like, the enormous kid in the class. I don't think she's grown an inch since then, but you should have seen how much taller she was than everyone else in our grade! We used to call her all kinds of names. And those glasses? I mean, what is her mother thinking, letting her walk outside with those things?"

Kayla felt relieved that the conversation had shifted away from her and her possible crush on Tom. "Well, but here's the funny thing," she said. "Matilda *works* at that shop, and she said I should bring you guys in, and that she has all kinds of cool stuff there that you might want to check out."

"As if," sniffed Alice.

"Yeah, as if," agreed Jess.

Kayla laughed. "Yeah, I didn't think you'd want to go. I did notice that they sell love potions there, though."

Alice turned toward Kayla and regarded her thoughtfully. "*Really*," she said. "Love potions, huh? As in, if we gave some to Nick and Scott and Anthony and Tom, they'd fall head over heels for us?"

Kayla nodded, ignoring her friend's mention of Tom, and smiled uncertainly. Alice didn't really believe the love potion would work, did she?

"We could totally spike the punch at your party!" said Jess eagerly.

"And get our crushes to drink it and then have them fall totally, madly in love with us!" added Pria breathlessly.

"Um, sure, I guess that's the idea," said Kayla, because she felt like they were waiting for her to say something.

The three girls waited while Alice considered the issue. "We'll go there tomorrow," she said.

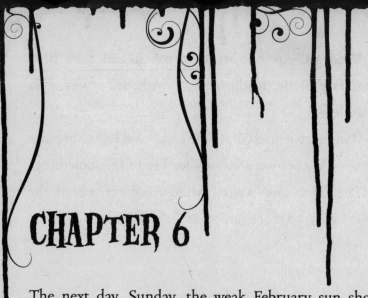

CHAPTER 6

The next day, Sunday, the weak February sun shone down on the girls as they made their way toward the mystical shop. The wind had died down completely, making it feel considerably warmer than the day before.

"What if it isn't open?" asked Jess.

Alice snorted. "Eleven o'clock on a weekend morning? What business wouldn't be open?"

But when they got to the shop, a CLOSED sign was hanging on the inside of the door. The girls stood there, looking at it.

"Let's go," said Pria, shivering. "This place kind of gives me the creeps anyway."

Suddenly the door was flung open, causing all four girls to jump back.

Matilda poked her head out. Her bangs half obscured her face, and much of what wasn't hidden by bangs was covered with her huge glasses. The sun glinted off them, making it impossible to see her eyes. "Oh, it's you," she said, waving them inside. "Come on in. I'm just opening up."

The girls exchanged glances with one another. Then Alice shrugged and led the way into the shop.

"I'm Alice Grafton, and this is Pria Patel and—"

"I know who you are," interrupted Matilda. "We've been classmates since fifth grade."

"Oh, right, I forgot all about that," said Alice, in a mock-sweet voice.

There was an awkward silence. Kayla hated awkward silences. She tried to think of something, anything, to say. Then she spotted Jinx sitting on the counter near the back register, grooming his hind leg. The front leg that had been hurt was now bandaged.

"Hey, how's Jinx doing?" she asked Matilda.

Matilda crossed her arms. "He's shipshape. The vet fixed up his leg. And I put a healing crystal on his collar, and he's right as rain now."

Pria snickered, but changed to a throat-clear when Matilda jerked her head to look at her sharply.

Kayla had to agree that Matilda did say some pretty strange things. *What seventh grader uses expressions like "ship-shape" and "right as rain"?* she thought.

"I'm glad he's better," she said, walking back toward the cat and reaching out a hand to stroke him. The cat started to purr.

"So Kayla says you guys sell love potions here," said Alice, getting straight to the point. "Is that true?"

Matilda lifted her chin a little and peered at Alice through her thick glasses, her bangs parting. "That's right," she said. "We've got all kinds of great things here—love potions, complexion creams, beauty elixirs . . ."

"Well if *you* work here," said Alice, "why haven't you used them? I mean, well, especially the beauty products . . ." She trailed off with a little snort and winked at Jess and Pria, who both laughed out loud. Kayla cringed. Did Alice really have to be so mean?

Matilda's face darkened, just for a moment, but then she smiled rather sweetly at Alice. "If you don't believe me, try this free sample," she said, hurrying around the back counter and stooping down below the register to rummage around in a drawer.

Kayla couldn't help noticing that Matilda moved

oddly. She swayed back and forth as though both her feet hurt to walk on them. She came back bearing a small silver plate with a pile of flat green disks on it. They were so bright, Kayla wondered if they would glow in the dark.

"What are those?" Jess asked suspiciously. She looked at them and wrinkled her nose.

"Wonder mints," said Matilda. "Guaranteed to make your hair shiny and your complexion totally blemish free." She smiled quickly, and Kayla caught a glimpse of a silver side tooth.

"Like I need *that*!" said Alice, flipping away a strand of her shiny hair.

Matilda leaned toward Alice, scrutinizing the side of her face closely. "Poppycock! You do indeed," she said. "I think I see a blemish coming out on your cheek there. Not to worry, though. One of these mints will clear it right up before it even appears."

Alice scowled at Matilda and reached for a mint. Jess and Pria followed. Kayla considered not taking one, and then put a hand up to feel her own hair, decidedly not shiny and sorely in need of smoothing. And her complexion? She could practically feel her chin breaking out. She reached out to take a mint.

But Matilda snatched the dish away before Kayla could take one. "Not for you," she said curtly. "*Your* hair is beyond the help of any wonder mint."

The other three girls laughed. Kayla tried not to let the comment bother her, but Matilda's words stung. She already felt like the least attractive girl in this group and was constantly wondering why they tolerated her presence in their elite circle. Her thick hair was hopelessly wavy, resembling the ripples on the surface of a pond. Kayla looked at Pria's glossy raven-black hair and dark eyes rimmed with thick lashes, then at Jess's princess-like features and straight, shining hair, and finally at Alice, who really did look like a model.

Kayla managed to smile as though she didn't care a bit, even though she really did. She wanted one of those mints.

The other three girls sucked on the mints. "These are actually pretty tasty," said Alice. "And I don't even *like* mint."

"How long before it takes effect?" asked Jess.

"Oh, you'll know when it does," said Matilda with a half smile.

"Okay, so how about that love potion?" said Alice. "Valentine's Day is coming up."

Matilda crossed her arms. "An empty wagon makes a lot of noise," she muttered.

"What did you just say?" asked Alice sharply.

"Never mind," said Matilda. "Why do you want a love potion? Anyone in particular you have your eye on?"

Alice's eyebrows shot up, but she didn't seem otherwise perturbed. "Maybe. Why do you care? Believe me, he's out of your league." Matilda just glowered at her in response. Alice let out an exasperated sigh. "So are you going to sell us the potion or not?" Her pretty face furrowed into a frown. She did not like to be kept waiting.

"Hang on. I'll see what we have," said Matilda, heading once more toward the back of the shop. This time she passed through the heavy velvet curtain. Alice, Pria, and Jess all looked at one another and burst into laughter. Kayla was sure Matilda could hear it.

"She is so *weird*," whispered Pria. "Did she really say 'poppycock' earlier?"

Jess and Alice giggled harder. Kayla managed a wan smile. She was getting a creepy-crawly feeling down her spine. All she wanted to do was get out of this shop. Out of the corner of her eye, she saw something glinting green, moving down the red wall behind Jess. She jumped, startled. It couldn't be. But it was: a huge green beetle, which stopped crawling and waggled one of its long antennae at her. Could it be one of the bugs that had been taken from Mr. Talbert's terrarium? Kayla darted a look at the other girls. They hadn't seen it. The bug continued on its way down the wall and disappeared behind Jess. Kayla shuddered.

She was still trying to think of a reason to lure her friends out of the shop when Matilda returned, carrying a small bottle made of thick glass. "Right. Love potion. Here it is. It's yours for only ninety-nine dollars, plus tax."

Kayla gulped.

"You have *got* to be joking," said Alice.

"I never joke," said Matilda in an icy tone. Kayla believed her.

"Ninety-nine *dollars*? For a dumb potion that's probably just grape juice or something? No way. There is no way we are paying that much. No wonder this dump has no customers. What a rip-off!" Alice picked up her bag and slung it onto her shoulder. She gestured to the other girls to follow her out of the store.

Matilda shrugged. "Suit yourself. The stuff really

44

works, just so you know. But I understand if you're reluctant to use it. It's pretty powerful. It'll make your crush act like an idiot, following you around like a lovesick puppy. But who needs *that* aggravation, right?"

She turned around and headed back toward the velvet curtain. Kayla could practically see the wheels turning in Alice's head. She knew what Alice must be thinking. Nearly every guy acted like a puppy around her, on a regular basis. Every guy except one: Nick Maroulis. He seemed as vain and self-centered as Alice, acting like she should be following *him* around. Kayla knew Alice well enough to know that she didn't like it when things didn't go the way she, Alice, wanted them to, and she was used to getting her way. Maybe this potion was worth a shot.

"Wait!" said Alice.

Matilda stopped, her back to them, and stood there quietly.

"We'll pay it. I fully realize that you are ripping us off big-time, but I want to see if it really works. We'll each contribute twenty-five dollars."

"Alice," said Kayla, the words coming out in a whisper from the side of her mouth, "I don't have a crush,

45

remember? I'd rather not chip in." She plunged her hand into her jeans pocket. She could feel a nickel and two pennies, and a carefully folded ten that her mother had given her, which she hadn't spent at the mall yesterday. She planned to give it back to her mother, who could definitely use it.

"I totally don't believe you," said Alice. "I totally think you do have a crush on someone, and you're just not telling us. Whatever." She turned to Jess and Pria. "You guys can give me thirty dollars each. I'll pay the rest." She shot a look at Kayla and pulled out her shiny, slender wallet.

Matilda was grinning beneath her bangs as Alice handed over a gold credit card. She moved behind the register. "You'll be happy you did it," she said, tapping expertly at the keypad.

"Hmph," said Alice, taking the money from Jess and Pria. "For a hundred dollars, it had better work."

"Now, listen carefully," said Matilda. "The potion needs fifteen minutes to take effect." As she spoke, she carefully wrapped the bottle in packing paper and then placed it into a velvet drawstring bag. "That's assuming you get the proportions right, which I advise you to pay attention to. Read the instructions I've included in the bag. You definitely do not want to mess up the dosage. After you administer the potion, you have to keep your beloved talking to you the whole time. Make sure he's making constant eye contact with you. Otherwise he'll fall for the wrong person!" She cackled.

Alice took the bag from Matilda with a small jerk and gestured with her chin to the rest of the girls to follow her out the door.

"Make sure you get the proportions right!" Matilda called after them.

"Yeah, okay, thanks, whatever," said Alice, more to the other girls than to Matilda.

As the door closed, Kayla once again heard laughter. Nasty, mocking laughter.

CHAPTER 7

The days flew by, and school passed in a blur. Kayla immersed herself in her schoolwork, but she couldn't stop thinking about Matilda. Fairbridge Middle was a big school, a combination of the four elementary schools, so it was possible to go days without seeing a particular person. On Wednesday she caught a glimpse of Matilda in the hallway near the science classrooms. Kayla had been about to walk into Mr. Talbert's room when Matilda came slowly down the hall, lumbering side to side with her curious gait, seemingly oblivious to the crowds of kids pushing past her. Was that a paper airplane that someone had just thrown into her hair? But Matilda just kept on walking. Her thick bangs were brushed straight down over her face, and her small mouth was turned up slightly in a smile.

That isn't a friendly smile, Kayla thought. *More like a grimace.*

Kayla was so distracted in science that day that she could barely concentrate on the fact that she and Tom Butler had been assigned to be lab partners. Ordinarily, her heart would be pounding and her face flushed. But she just stared down at the Bunsen burner, seeing Matilda's face reflected in the narrow blue flame.

"Um, Earth to Kayla?" said Tom, giving her a little nudge with his elbow.

"Sorry," she said, shaking herself from her thoughts. "Do you want to heat the zinc and alloy powders and I'll do the graphing, or the other way around?"

He put his chin in his hand and looked at her, as though studying a puzzling abstract painting. "Well, I suppose I *could*, but the alloy lab was *last* week. We might have more success if we do *today's* lab, which is about the law of conservation of mass."

Kayla blew away a strand of hair and rolled her eyes. "Sorry. I'm a little distracted, I guess."

"Ya think?" he said, but in a nice way.

"So, um, are you going to Alice's party Saturday night?" she asked, trying to sound casual as she poured out a beaker of vinegar.

"Not sure yet," he said. "I hear they're predicting a big snowstorm. And I'm not a big party guy. I'll make it a game day decision, I guess."

Tom pulled out a piece of graph paper and began drawing lines with his pencil and ruler.

"So . . . how about you?" he asked just as casually.

"What *about* me?"

"Are you going? To Alice's party?" Tom was a lefty, and as he drew the lines, his left elbow grazed Kayla's hand.

She felt an electric current race through her whole arm, and her heart rate quickened. Why did she have such a big crush on this goofy-looking guy? His ears stuck out. And those huge feet!

"Yeah, I'll be there," she said with a grin. "You know Alice. She plans exciting parties. Never a dull moment when she's in the room." She sighed. "I'm going over there Saturday afternoon to help her choose which one of her seventeen outfit options to wear."

He grinned. "She's into clothes, I guess, huh."

"You might say," said Kayla. "But she's nice and stuff."

"Yeah, I guess."

They were silent for a minute.

"Maybe I'll tag along with my cousin," he said.

"Cool," she said, smiling shyly.

"Cool," he replied.

Saturday afternoon, Kayla's mom dropped her off at the Graftons' house.

"Oh, by the way, when I talked to Alice's mom yesterday," her mother began, as Kayla climbed into the backseat to get out.

Kayla stopped and looked back at her mother. "Oh. You talked to her? Not e-mailed?"

"No, I actually had a real conversation," said her mother wryly. "She invited me to the party tonight. It seems that a lot of the parents will be there, having their own party upstairs. I didn't think I could possibly find a babysitter for your little brothers tonight, it being Valentine's Day and all. But as luck would have it, Taylor Haskins next door is grounded, so her mother said that Taylor would be delighted to babysit."

Kayla swallowed. "That's great, Mom." She cringed to think of all those parents hearing her mother's accent.

Her mother smiled. "Honey, I know you're embarrassed by me."

"No! Mom! No, I'm not. I—"

"It's okay, I don't mind," she said. "It's a twelve-year-old's job to be embarrassed by her mother. But don't worry. I promise not to go downstairs. I'll pretend I don't even know you. Anyway, I'm just going to put in an appearance and leave as soon as possible. The moment Caroline Grafton remembered that I work in admissions at the Academy, she suddenly started being so much nicer to me."

Kayla thought about what Matilda had said, about how Kayla's friends were thinking along those same lines. She put the thought out of her head. No, they were her friends. They liked her for who she was, not the school they thought her mother could get them into.

CHAPTER 8

Alice was in the kitchen with her mother when Kayla knocked and then let herself in through the side door a few seconds later.

"Hey, Kay," said Alice, as Kayla stomped her boots and then placed them neatly along the wall next to the other boots.

"Alice, I want you to remove all these boots before the party and put them in the front hall closet," said her mother.

Alice rolled her eyes. "Whatever," she said.

"How are you, Kayley?" asked Mrs. Grafton, smiling at Kayla with her mouth but not her eyes.

Alice didn't correct her mother. *Maybe she didn't hear her mom say my name incorrectly,* Kayla thought.

"I'm fine, thanks," said Kayla. Mrs. Grafton looked about ten years younger than Kayla's mother, but Kayla suspected it was because she spent a lot of time at the beauty parlor and the gym.

"Jess and Pria are up in my room, trying on clothes," Alice said to Kayla. "Did you bring a bunch of outfits too?"

Kayla stared down at her outfit, which was visible through her open coat. She'd worn her black flippy skirt with the blue top that her cousin had just sent her. She loved the blue top. "I was going to wear this," she said. "I brought a pair of black flats to wear. They're in my bag."

"You look adorable, Kaitlin," said Mrs. Grafton. "How creative of you to put that outfit together. I had a nice chat with your mother, by the way. She has a charming accent. And to work at the academy! In admissions, no less! What an exciting job that must be!"

"Yes, she likes it," Kayla said. "This is a busy time of year for her, because all the applications for next year are in and they're reviewing them right now."

"How nice. I am so looking forward to visiting with her tonight!" Mrs. Grafton stepped onto a footstool and pulled a huge punch bowl down from a high shelf in the cupboard. She handed it down to Alice, who set it on the counter next to another large punch bowl. Kayla wondered why someone would own two large punch bowls. She was pretty sure her mom didn't own even one.

"Come upstairs," Alice commanded Kayla, taking her by the sleeve and pulling her across the kitchen. Kayla followed Alice down the hallway, glancing left into the enormous dining room, which flowed into the L-shaped living room. The cleaning lady had obviously been there. The wood surfaces gleamed, the upholstered furniture looked fluffed up as though it had just arrived from the furniture store, and the throw pillows were placed perfectly.

"We're supposed to put the coats in there," said Alice, pointing at the study across the hall.

Upstairs in Alice's bedroom, mounds of clothing were heaped on her canopied bed. More clothing had spilled onto the floor. Pria yelled hello from inside Alice's bathroom, where she and Jess were slathering green paste on their cheeks.

"We're doing facials!" called Pria. "Come join us!"

The bathroom was large enough for all four girls to fit comfortably. One wall was mirrored, and the long counter included side-by-side sinks. Kayla pulled her thick hair back into a ponytail and then took the tube of facial stuff from Pria and began slathering it on her own face.

"What are you going to do about your hair, Kay?" asked Alice as she, too, began swirling the green paste onto her face.

"Nothing, I guess," said Kayla. "I was thinking I'd just wear it down."

Alice sighed. "You should try something different. You just have to put a little effort into it. You could be halfway decent-looking, you know, if you tried a little harder."

"Thanks," said Kayla. Why was it she always felt worse, not better, when Alice complimented her?

"Those green wafers that weird girl gave us *so* did not work," said Jess crossly, looking at her green-masked face in the mirror. It was drying and starting to crack. "I am totally breaking out on my forehead."

Kayla glanced at Jess's skin, which was as smooth as porcelain. She'd never once seen a breakout on her face.

"Has your mom finished making the punch yet?"

asked Pria. She leaned over the sink and began scrubbing off her dried mask.

"She's working on it now," said Alice. "It'll be so cool if this potion works."

"Did you read the instructions?" asked Kayla worriedly. "Matilda said to be careful with the proportions."

Alice gave her a look. "What do you care, Kay? You didn't chip in for it, remember?"

Why wouldn't Alice just drop it? Kayla began to stammer. "I—I don't have a crush."

"As if," said Alice. "You totally like Tom. And with the hair day you appear to be having, it can't hurt to hand him a big glass of the punch, assuming he shows up tonight."

Kayla looked at herself in the mirror. With her green face and untidy ponytail, and tendrils of hair spiking out around her face, she had to agree with Alice. Maybe she *should* get Tom to drink some.

After their facials, the girls had a makeup session. Alice made Kayla her project, expertly applying products with about seventeen different brushes. Kayla had to admit,

Alice was really talented. She looked at herself in the mirror.

"Wow, I look pretty good," she said. Her brown eyes were rimmed with a smoky purple that made them look enormous, and her mascaraed lashes looked thick and lustrous.

"I had no idea you had such long eyelashes, Kay," said Jess, with more than a little jealousy in her tone. "They look like false eyelashes, they're so big!"

Kayla smiled, admiring the sparkly glints on her eyelids. "Thanks," she said.

"So do you think people will come?" asked Pria. "I mean, the weather is supposed to be pretty awful tonight. It looks like it's going to start snowing soon."

Alice's face darkened. "They'll come!" she snapped. "It's not supposed to start snowing until later."

"Yes, right, I'm sure they will," said Pria quickly.

"The party doesn't start for another hour," said Alice. "Why don't we make some prank calls?"

Jess and Pria squealed and jumped up and down.

"I know how to block the caller's name so the other person can't tell who's calling them," said Jess eagerly.

"Duh, everyone knows how to do that," said Alice.

"You say such obvious things sometimes, Jess. Maybe we should have bought some intelligence potion from that girl Matilda too."

Jess drooped.

"Just joking," said Alice sweetly, clasping Jess's arm and skipping with her into the bedroom.

They took turns calling Nick, Scott, and Anthony, masking their voices and asking the boys who they liked, then hanging up and shrieking with laughter. Kayla laughed along with them, although she wasn't exactly sure what was so funny.

None of the boys said much. They probably knew who was on the other end.

"Your turn," said Alice, turning to Kayla. "Call Matilda. Pretend to be Tom, and ask her if she wants to go with you to my party."

Kayla's heart sank.

Pria and Jess looked at each other and gasped. "Oh that is *so evil*, Alice!" said Jess excitedly.

"I know!" Alice smiled, pleased with herself. "What's her last name again?" She pulled her laptop into her lap and found a phone number website.

"I think it's Warner," said Pria.

Kayla held her breath, praying that Matilda's number would not be listed.

Alice typed in the name and frowned. "Great. There are, like, two dozen Warners in Fairbridge. Do you know her parents' names?"

Kayla shook her head, relieved. "Guess we can't call her," she said. She had an awful feeling in her stomach, as though she'd swallowed a heavy stone. She hated prank calling, making jokes at someone else's expense, especially someone as teased as Matilda. But she didn't dare speak up. She already felt like an outsider in this group.

"We'll call the shop," said Alice, typing in the business name, Esoterica. She grabbed Kayla's cell phone and punched in the number. "Here," she said. "If the owner answers, hang up. I put it on speaker."

Kayla took the phone, praying again, this time that no one would answer. That the phone would go straight to voice mail.

But Matilda answered after the second ring.

"Um, hello, Matilda?" said Kayla, pitching her voice low.

"Who's this?" Matilda asked suspiciously.

"It's Tom. Tom Butler. From school." Kayla's stomach was starting to twist into knots. "I was, uh, just wondering if you wanted to come to a party with me tonight."

"A party? Gosh golly gee. You mean the one at Alice Grafton's?"

"Uh, yeah. That party."

Kayla looked up to see the other three girls noiselessly laughing their heads off.

"I'd love to," said Matilda, to Kayla's surprise. "I work here until six o'clock. What time?"

"Uh, I'll uh, swing by the store then," said Kayla-as-Tom. "It's a short walk to her house from there."

"Okay, bye," said Matilda, and hung up.

As soon as Kayla clicked the phone off, the other three girls howled with laughter.

"I cannot *believe* she fell for it!" said Alice, dabbing the corner of her eye delicately so as not to smudge her makeup.

"This girl just keeps getting weirder!" exclaimed Pria. "Did she really say 'gosh golly gee'?"

"I think she did!" said Jess, still laughing.

"Come on. Let's go downstairs," said Alice. "People are going to start showing up in a few minutes. We can see how Mom is doing with the punch."

"I'll be down in a minute," said Kayla, looking for an excuse to be alone for a moment. "Got to go to the bathroom."

She watched the three girls leave the bedroom, then sat down heavily on Alice's bed. What had she done? She felt as though she might throw up.

She picked up her phone from the bed where she'd tossed it. She hit redial. She would call Matilda and figure out something to say.

The phone rang and rang, and then a machine picked up. It was Matilda's voice. *"You've reached Esoterica!"* she said in a breathy, dramatic tone. *"Mystical Magical Spells and Potions! Our store hours are—"*

Kayla closed her eyes and held the phone away from her ear. Now what? She put it back to her ear.

"—but leave a message at the beep and we'll get back to you." The phone beeped.

"Uh, hi, Matilda? This is Tom again," said Kayla, again pitching her voice low. "I just threw up, so . . . I guess I can't go to the party after all. So I won't be coming to pick you up at six. And anyway, it's probably going to be a boring party and stuff. It wouldn't have been fun. Sorry about that." She clicked off, and then fell backward on the bed. She closed her eyes and prayed Matilda would get the message.

Then her eyes flew open. She sat back up. Did hitting redial mean she hadn't masked the caller's number? Would Matilda see that it was Kayla who had called back, not Tom? She groaned and flopped back down. Aside from the fact that she hated playing tricks on people, she had a terrible feeling that Matilda was about the worst person to play a trick on. Matilda made her feel uneasy. The last thing she needed was to join the ranks of people Matilda considered her enemies.

The next thing Kayla knew, she heard a scream coming from downstairs.

CHAPTER 9

Kayla's eyes sprang open. She jumped up from the bed and raced out of the room. She must have fallen asleep after she dialed Matilda. She hurried down the thickly carpeted stairs, wondering where the scream had come from.

She burst into the kitchen and found Alice, surrounded by Mrs. Grafton, Pria, and Jess. Alice's father was leaning against the counter, checking his smartphone.

"Look, Kay!" shrieked Alice, dashing over to her and clutching a necklace she wore around her neck. "Daddy just gave it to me for Valentine's Day. Isn't it to die for?"

The necklace was a heart-shaped gold pendant, studded all around with diamonds. Kayla had no doubt they were real.

"Wow!" she said. "That's . . . that's really something." The thing must have cost as much as Kayla's mother made in a month. Or two.

"I know, right?" said Alice. She shrieked again and flung herself into her father's arms. "Thanks, Daddy!" she squealed.

"Hey! Careful, honey!" said her father, disentangling himself from her embrace. "You almost made me drop my phone, and I'm in the middle of an important business e-mail."

"Daddy is always in the middle of an important business e-mail," Alice said to her friends.

Mrs. Grafton was now all dressed up in a black blouse, skinny black pants, and rickety-looking high heels. Kayla could smell her expensive perfume from across the kitchen. Mrs. Grafton held up another piece of sparkly jewelry, which dangled above a satin-lined box. It looked like a diamond earring. "They're lovely, Miles," she said in a flat tone that sounded like she didn't think they were lovely at all. "Might be a bit heavy for my ears, though. I'm sure the jewelers will do an exchange."

Mr. Grafton looked up from his phone and glowered at her. "Glad to hear it," he said, and went back to his messages.

"So, Daddy, you'll be here for the party tonight, right?"

He looked up sharply. "What party? Is that what all this fuss is about?" He gestured around the kitchen at the platters of food.

Alice sighed patiently. "Yes, Daddy. It's my Valentine's party? Remember I told you? I invited a bunch of kids from school. Didn't you notice I'm wearing my new dress?" She did a little twirl, her perfect hair bouncing and the hem of her red dress flaring.

He glanced up at her dress and frowned. "Where's the rest of it?"

"The rest of what?"

"Your dress. It's a little short! Are boys coming?" he asked, furrowing his brow.

"Yes, Daddy!" She giggled. "But they're all leaving by eleven."

He grunted and looked back down at his phone, paging down the screen with his thumb. "I think you ought to cancel the party," he said abruptly. "They're predicting a big storm tonight. Could snow ten to fifteen inches, and it's supposed to start up any time now."

Alice's chin quivered, and Kayla was afraid she was

going to burst into tears. "It's not going to be that bad," she said in a pouty voice. "It's barely snowing out there."

"Really, Miles," said Mrs. Grafton. "Everything's all set. We're not going to cancel at the last minute. And anyway, everyone has four-wheel drive these days. What's a little snow?" She shot him an annoyed look, which appeared to be lost on him, as he had resumed typing on his smartphone.

Kayla thought about her mom's old minivan, and how it was definitely not good in the snow.

She was relieved when the doorbell rang a moment later. She followed Alice and the other girls to the front door to answer it.

It was a group of kids from school. They were followed by wave after wave of people, kids and parents, who streamed in, stomping their boots and handing over their coats, which the girls flung over the backs of the couches in the study.

As Kayla staggered toward the study with an armful of coats, she saw her mother step into the foyer. Mrs. Grafton stood by, ready to greet her.

"You must be Kayley's mother," Kayla heard Mrs. Grafton say. "You have the same hair. I can't believe we haven't met after all this time!"

"It's Kayla," said Kayla's mother drily. "And actually, we've met several times, Caroline. I'm Celeste Evans. Lovely to see you again."

"Oh, of course, Celeste!" said Mrs. Grafton. "What a charming accent you have!"

Kayla flinched. She moved toward the study, trying not to listen to more, but she heard her mother protesting that she was just there for a little while, that she had a babysitter at home and couldn't stay long. That was a relief.

"Let's go downstairs," said Alice, as Kayla rejoined the group of kids. Alice led them down to the basement.

Kayla had been in Alice's basement a few times before, but she was amazed at how transformed the place looked tonight. It was a huge, sprawling space, with a home theater; a game room with every game imaginable, including foosball, Ping-Pong, air hockey, pinball, and a pool table; and another large room with a hardwood floor that Kayla knew was usually used as Mrs. Grafton's exercise room. All the equipment had been rolled away to a corner of the room, so it was now a wide-open space with a karaoke machine already blaring popular dance songs. The place looked beautiful. Pria, Jess, and Alice had strung heart-shaped lights across every room, and red candles flickered on tables. On a table along the wall of the dance room sat a huge bowl of red punch.

Kayla felt left out, as she so often did. It looked like Jess and Pria had been there most of the day, helping with the party. Alice hadn't invited her to come that early.

"Did you put the stuff in?" Pria asked Alice, who, along with Jess, had just come up to stand with Kayla. She could speak in a normal tone of voice—there was no danger of being overheard over the music.

"I did the grown-ups' bowl already," Alice replied. "I figured my parents could use a little rekindling of their relationship tonight. All they do is fight." She grimaced.

"So when are you going to add the potion to our punch?" asked Jess eagerly. "Did you see? Anthony and Scott just showed up, and Nick is with them!"

"Yep, I saw," said Alice, fluffing up her beautiful hair with her manicured hands. "I'm going to do ours right now. We can pour it in, hand everyone a cup at the same time, and then propose a toast."

"I wonder how it works with grown-ups," mused Pria as the girls huddled around the punch bowl and watched Alice pour the rest of the contents of the vial in. "I mean, Matilda said it takes fifteen minutes to take effect, and you have to be talking to your crush the whole time. What if they're, like, talking to someone else's parent? Ew!"

"I put extra into theirs," said Alice. "That way it will speed up the process. Usually the husband goes and fetches the wife a drink first thing, so I'm sure the right couples will be standing together when the punch takes effect."

Kayla felt a jolt of alarm but said nothing. What if her mother was still up there? What if Mr. Grafton gave her some punch? She shuddered. No, her mother seemed like she only wanted to say hi and then get out of there. She'd probably left already.

Alice, Jess, and Pria were now moving around from person to person, handing out cups full of punch.

"Don't drink yet!" Alice shouted to each person over the music. "We're going to have a toast!"

Alice thrust a cup of punch into Kayla's hands. "Technically you don't really deserve this," she said. "I should punish you for not helping us buy the potion."

"Well, thanks," said Kayla, taking the cup.

"And don't try to say you didn't help because you don't have a crush," snapped Alice. Her icy blue eyes flashed.

As Alice moved away, Kayla darted a look around, searching for Tom. He hadn't come. She sighed and set down her cup.

She watched Alice chatting and laughing with Nick Maroulis. She could see by the way he turned his shoulders slightly away from her, and by the distracted look on his face, that he wasn't all that enthusiastic about Alice's attention. *How can that be?* she wondered. Was he really not interested in Alice, the most gorgeous and popular girl in the seventh grade? Or was he just so self-absorbed that he wasn't interested in anything besides basketball and his hair?

She felt someone touch her shoulder, and turned.

"Hey," said Tom. "I decided to show up. After all, you promised an exciting party."

CHAPTER 10

"Tom!" cried Alice, rushing over to him. She took his arm and didn't so much as glance at Kayla. "I didn't think you were coming! What's wrong with your foot?"

Tom grinned that sideways smile Kayla loved so much. "Sprained my ankle in basketball practice yesterday," he said, holding out his bandaged left foot. "It's not that bad, Coach says, but I'm not supposed to put any weight on it for a few days."

Kayla noticed he had a single crutch.

"Nice going, klutzo!" Alice giggled, giving Tom a little shove to the chest. "Why do you even play basketball? I mean, it's not like you're very tall—no offense."

Tom grinned. "No offense taken. But I do play pretty good *offense*."

Kayla smiled a little at his joke, but Alice didn't seem to get it. "Come over here. There's a chair you can sit in."

She led him across the room toward where Nick and Scott and Anthony were standing awkwardly in a clump, holding their punch cups. Kayla watched as Alice pushed Tom down into a chair next to the table and then ladled out some punch for him and put the cup into his hands. He glanced back at Kayla and gave her a little smile and a shrug.

"She's trying to make Nick jealous," said Pria, who was suddenly standing next to her. Kayla hadn't known she was there.

Pria nodded miserably. "She was just flirting like crazy with Scott, too. Isn't it enough that all the rest of the seventh-grade boys already like her? Does she have to go and flirt with *our* crushes too?"

Kayla was excited that Pria was opening up to her—maybe she and Jess were getting a little tired of Alice's attitude too. But before she could say anything, a voice boomed out loud and clear.

"Attention, everyone!"

Across the room, Alice motioned to Tom to stand up from his chair. Then she turned the music down and climbed onto his empty chair. Everyone stopped talking to listen. Kids from the other room put down their Ping-Pong paddles and pool cues and filed into the room. *Alice looks beautiful*, Kayla thought. She seemed to grow more radiant simply by being stared at. Her perfectly cut, close-fitting red dress accentuated her slim figure and her long, toned legs, which were somewhere between supermodel and superathlete. Kayla looked at the boys, most of whom were standing together in one group. It was true. They were all obsessed with Alice. Who wouldn't be? *Even Tom seems dazzled by her beauty*, she thought miserably.

"I would like to make a Valentine's Day toast!" Alice started to say. "Everyone raise your glass!"

A vision of Matilda's face flashed before Kayla. She remembered the gleam in her eyes behind those thick glasses as she'd talked about the potion. Everyone was raising a cup.

"You too, Kayla!" commanded Alice from across the room.

Kayla realized that everyone in the room was looking at her. She picked up the cup she'd set down earlier and raised it along with everyone else. Everyone drank.

Kayla put the cup to her lips and took a tiny sip. It tasted bad and reminded her a bit of medicine.

She spat the punch back into her cup and set it down on the table. Her mouth felt all tingly and numb. Something was definitely not right, though no one else seemed to mind the bitter, numbing taste, or else they were too scared to insult Alice.

Across the room, she noticed Tom, who was chatting away with Nick and still holding his cup. Had he had any punch?

"Tom! You didn't drink any yet!" she heard Alice say, and watched her jump down from her chair, light as a cat. Kayla watched Tom raise his cup to his lips.

In two bounds Kayla had crossed the room, bumping into several people as she did so. Tom didn't even see her coming. A second later she'd knocked the cup from his hand and onto the floor. Tom almost toppled over with surprise.

The room fell silent, except for the music, which someone had turned back up.

Tom blinked at the spreading puddle of red punch on the off-white carpet. Then he looked at Kayla, his eyebrows raised in a question.

Kayla didn't dare look at Alice. "Did you drink some?" she said to Tom.

"Uh, yeah, I did. It's pretty good," he said.

She turned to Alice. "I'm so sorry about the carpet," she said, although her voice felt pinched and thin, the way it sometimes does in a dream when you're trying to scream and find you can't. "It was an accident. I'll go get something to clean it up."

"*Look* at the carpet!" she heard Alice say as Kayla bounded up the stairs to the kitchen. But all Kayla was thinking about was seeing if her mother was still at the party. She had to make sure her mother had left—and if she was still there, that she didn't drink any of that disgusting punch.

CHAPTER 11

Kayla burst into the kitchen. It was oddly quiet. Through the large window over the sink, she could glimpse the snow coming down. It looked like it had finally started to snow heavily.

She crossed the kitchen and went through the swinging door that led to the large, open pantry. Still not a soul to be seen. Where was everyone?

At the other end of the pantry was an open doorway that led into the large dining and living rooms. A man was leaning against the doorjamb with his back to her, probably chatting quietly with someone next to him that she couldn't see. She could hear music playing. Not the same kind of music they were playing downstairs, but it was reassuring to see that people were in there.

She stepped across the pantry and stood behind the man. He was a large man; she had no idea whose dad he was, but he certainly took up most of the doorway.

"Excuse me?" she said tentatively. "Um, sir? Can I just squeeze by you?" Her voice came out sounding high and barely audible.

The man didn't budge.

Kayla's fear for her mother made her bolder than usual. "Sir, I just need to . . ." She put a firm hand on his arm and tried to guide him over to the side of the doorway, so she could squeeze past.

For a strange moment the man felt weightless. Then, with a sickening feeling, she realized he was falling. Falling over. Over to the side, in the direction she had nudged him ever so gently.

Kayla screamed, or tried to. Instead of a scream, a strangled, unearthly sound came out of her throat. The man toppled over like a tall tree beneath a woodsman's ax. She tried to shriek again, several times, in rapid, gulping succession, but the sounds came out as mere squeaks, and then she couldn't seem to make any sound at all. She stared in horror at the man lying on the carpet, the crystal punch cup in his hand, his eyes open but unseeing.

For a moment she couldn't take her eyes off the cup, which hadn't broken on the thick carpet. With the red punch stain next to him, seeping under his face, which was turned to the side, he looked . . . dead. But he couldn't be dead. He was still breathing, although it was barely noticeable.

"I'm—I'm so sorry, sir!" she tried to say, but no sound came out of her mouth. Her tongue felt thick and uncooperative, as though she'd just left the dentist after a major round of Novocain.

She raised her eyes to look around the room. She froze and staggered backward, nearly falling.

Eight or nine parents were in the room. Some were clustered around the table, which was filled with platters of food, drinks, and the large punch bowl in the center of it. Several others were standing around the outer area of the room, in little groups. No one was moving. No one was speaking. Everyone was still as a statue, frozen in mid-gesture. One man held the ladle of the punch bowl suspended above his other hand, which held a crystal punch cup, as though he'd been frozen mid-pour. A woman had one arm raised halfway to her open mouth, a small finger sandwich in her hand.

Kayla was suddenly struck by the memory of an experience she'd had when she was a little girl. She and her father had been hiking together on a wintry day, she in her little pink plastic kiddie snowshoes, and he in his grown-up trekking gear. They were on a trip north together, she couldn't remember why, and he'd wanted to show her one of his favorite places from his boyhood. She'd been amazed by the snow and the cold, having lived all her life in Texas. And then they'd come rather suddenly upon a brook. She'd stopped and stared at the waterfall, which had frozen in a perfect ice sculpture of its watery state; it looked as though a wizard had waved his wand and stopped the rushing waterfall instantaneously.

She blinked her eyes, hoping and praying that she was just imagining things. That she was the one who had gone crazy, not the whole world. But the people remained as still as statues, the cheerful music sounding almost mocking in that terrible room.

Her mother. Sudden, wild terror clutched her heart. She had to see if her mother was here. Hadn't she said she'd just stay a few minutes? Hadn't she said she'd leave as soon as she could? Kayla stepped to the window, which overlooked the front yard and the sweeping driveway, to see if she could find their battered old minivan. Outside the snow was swirling thickly. It was impossible to see past the arc of the floodlight, and the parked cars she could see were already blanketed with a thick coating of snow. It was impossible to tell whether her mom's minivan was one of them.

She hurried past the frozen people in the dining room, taking great care not to touch them, and into the large living room.

More frozen grown-ups. At least a dozen. She recognized both Pria's and Jess's mothers. They were sitting on the sofa together. Mrs. Patel's mouth was open, as though she was chatting, but she didn't move. Several others stood in clumps, looking like someone had taken a still photograph of a lively conversation. There was Mr. Grafton, Alice's father, standing in a corner, frozen in mid-tap over his smartphone. He looked like a mannequin in a men's store. There was Mrs. Grafton, standing with a woman Kayla didn't know, gesturing to a fancy Chinese-looking vase on a side table. Kayla tried to wail with horror, but her throat had closed up, as though she was being partially strangled.

She had to find her mother or be absolutely certain she wasn't here. If she hadn't been so desperate to find her, Kayla would have been more focused on trying to figure out what could possibly be going on. After all, people didn't just freeze like statues. For now, though, she just wanted to find—or actually not find—her mother.

She made her way through the room and then across the hall in front of the central staircase. She walked into the study, where they'd piled all the coats. No one seemed to be in there. She turned and looked back across the hall into the living room, at the horrible, frozen figures. She took a tiny step back, stumbled, and fell, coming very close to bashing her head on the coffee table. As she lay sprawled on the floor, she looked up.

Her mother was sitting on the couch, almost buried by mounds of coats. She had her coat on and was leaning down, as though in the middle of fastening her boot. And like all the others, she was frozen.

Kayla tried to shout, moan, cry, anything, but once again no sound came out of her mouth. She scrambled to her hands and knees and stood up shakily. She reached out a hand to touch her mother. Her mother's cheek was warm, her eyes bright but unseeing. She wasn't dead. *A dead person wouldn't feel warm. Right?* she reasoned to herself desperately.

Her phone. She would dial 911. She pulled it out to make the call and then remembered. She couldn't speak. Should she dial it anyway? She'd seen a movie once where a person who was tied up and gagged managed to dial 911. Even without hearing anyone speak, the operator had sent help based on the location of the call. But what could they possibly do when they got here? People didn't just freeze. They wouldn't know what to do or how this had happened.

How did *this happen?* Kayla wondered. Her mind was rapidly calculating, and then it stopped. She knew the answer. It had to have been the punch—it had frozen everyone who drank it. That was why she couldn't speak. She'd taken a sip and spat it out. So she wasn't frozen, but the punch had somehow paralyzed her throat and voice.

Kayla tried to remain calm. Had she swallowed any of it? If even a tiny drop had found its way down her throat and was now coursing through her system, she could be moments away from becoming frozen herself.

In a sudden flashback, she remembered how just a

few days ago she'd wished her mother would lose her voice, so that Kayla wouldn't be embarrassed by her mother's accent. She closed her eyes, trying to blot out the guilt.

She hurried into the kitchen and back toward the door leading down to the basement, filled with dread. If people upstairs were frozen, what would she find when she went downstairs? What if she was the only person in the house who could still move? She had to go down there and find out.

She put a hand on the basement door. Then she heard a movement behind her in the kitchen. She whirled around.

CHAPTER 12

Bulbous black eyes. A smushed-in face. Flopped-over ears. A ridiculous curled tail.

Buttercup.

Kayla let out her breath and realized she'd been holding it for quite some time. The dog stared up at her questioningly. He was probably as freaked out as she was. Even though she'd noticed that his saggy face always seemed to have a worried expression on it, the worry was more pronounced than usual now. While he'd never shown much interest in her before, he was wagging his tail ever so slightly, as though seeking reassurance from her, the only other being who seemed to be mobile in that terrible house. Grimly she leaned down and patted his head, and then she opened the door and headed down to the basement.

The stairs creaked as she inched down each one. She couldn't yet see any kids—frozen or otherwise—but she could hear the music from the karaoke machine blaring and nothing more. That same eerie almost-silence she had experienced upstairs.

She was halfway down the stairs when the lights went out.

If she'd been able to, Kayla would have begun to whimper. But no sounds came from her mouth. The music stopped. The basement was suddenly plunged into darkness. There was no sound. No talking. No movement.

At least it wasn't pitch black. Alice had put several candles around the room, red for Valentine's Day, and they cast an eerie, flickering light on the people standing around the room. As Kayla had suspected, everyone was frozen.

She picked up a candle from the table and moved through the room, the flickering flame dimly illuminating one frozen person after another.

There was Alice, her elbows raised above her head, her hands frozen mid-fluff; she'd been running her hands through her hair at the moment she froze. She was standing in the middle of a group of boys, all frozen—she recognized Patrick Morley, Eric Ishak, Andrew Trevenen, Jason Yan. They stared down at her with their unblinking eyes.

There were Jess and Pria, standing close to each other, Jess with her hand cupped next to Pria's ear, as though stopped in mid-whisper.

There was Nick, standing with Scott and Anthony. Nick was half turned toward the mirrored wall of shelves over the bar area, and Kayla noticed he was flexing his bicep, as though he'd been frozen just as he was checking himself out.

Where was Tom? Was he one of these still, shadowy figures? He'd definitely sipped the punch. She hadn't gotten to him in time. And no doubt Alice had refilled his punch cup after Kayla had gone upstairs. Kayla moved through the eerie room with its motionless figures, its flickering candles, and went into the next room, where the movie had been running—Alice had carefully picked out goopy love stories, although from the looks of the several frozen kids sitting in the audience, people had been chatting over, rather than watching, the movie. She made her way carefully into the game room. Several kids—all boys, it seemed—were frozen in various positions, holding pool cues, video game controllers, or twirling foosball handles. But no Tom. Where was he?

A sob rose in her throat and stayed there. She felt like it might strangle her. She had to think, think, think.

She had to find Matilda.

She had to find Matilda and make her do something, give Kayla something, to undo this terrible curse, or whatever it was. But how would she find her? She had no idea where Matilda lived, and she remembered how many Warners there had been in the directory. Kayla couldn't call her anyway—not without a voice.

She'd go to the shop. She could walk there. Maybe, just maybe, she'd find Matilda there. Or the owner of the shop, who might know what to do, or at least how to find Matilda. Then a worried thought popped into her head: What were the chances of someone being at the shop at nine p.m. on a Saturday night, in the middle of a terrible snowstorm? She dismissed the thought. Going to the store and looking for Matilda was her only hope.

She made her way toward the foot of the basement steps, groping her way around frozen people, trying not to touch anyone.

Then she felt a hand on her shoulder.

CHAPTER 13

She screamed soundlessly, almost dropping the candle, and whirled around.

"Kayla!"

It was Tom. Even in the light of the flickering candle, she could see his pale face, his wild eyes filled with horror.

"What's happening?" he croaked. "The last thing I remember is you going up those stairs, and people talking and Alice bugging out about the stain on the carpet and how her mom was going to be so mad. She poured me more punch, and I chugged down the whole cup because I was so thirsty, and then I can't remember anything. It was like when the cable goes out for a second and the TV screen goes black. And then"—he was breathing heavily, on the verge of hyperventilating—"and then I guess I sort of came to, and the lights were out and everyone was, well, like this." He gestured toward the frozen kids. "Why aren't you that way? Why am I not that way? Is it a gas leak or something?"

Kayla put a hand on his arm, and then pointed to her mouth and shook her head.

"You can't talk? Why can't you talk?" His voice was climbing in pitch.

She took his arm and indicated that they should go upstairs to the kitchen where there was at least a little light coming in through the window.

He nodded and gripped his crutch, then climbed the stairs, leaning heavily on the banister as he limped on his bad ankle.

As they emerged into the dim, gloomy kitchen, Buttercup charged toward them, barking his head off. Then he stopped barking abruptly, as though he'd suddenly remembered who they were. He plopped down on his belly, his little legs splayed out in front and behind. He put his head down on his front paws and began whimpering.

Kayla took out her phone, opened her notepad app, and began typing furiously:

CAN'T TALK. WE NEED TO FIND HELP. CAN YOU CALL 911?

Tom read the note. He nodded and picked up the cordless phone on the counter. He put it back down in the cradle. "It's dead, duh. There's no power. I left my cell down in the basement somewhere. Give me yours."

She handed it over to him. He stared down at the screen, then looked at her. "No service. Since when is there no service in this neighborhood?"

Kayla shrugged, as if to say she had no idea.

"Must be the storm," he muttered. "We could go outside and knock on the neighbors' doors, but how could they help? They're out of power too, so their phones won't work either. Kayla, what do we do?"

Kayla took her phone back and began typing again. I'LL GO FOR HELP. YOU STAY HERE AND SEE IF THERE'S ANYTHING YOU CAN DO TO HELP THESE PEOPLE. MAYBE THEY'LL WAKE UP SOON?

Tom read it and said, "I'll go. Let me."

Kayla shook her head and pointed at his ankle.

"Stupid ankle. Okay, you'll have to go."

She typed again and shoved the phone toward him. DO YOU KNOW ANYTHING ABOUT MATILDA WARNER?

"Matilda?" His eyes widened. "Yeah, that's weird that

91

you should mention her, because she came to my house tonight. Knocked on the door, and when I answered, she said something bizarre about being sorry I was sick. I told her I wasn't sick. I guess someone had prank called her and pretended to be me."

Kayla typed again. WHAT HAPPENED? IT'S IMPORTANT! TELL ME!

"I invited her in. My parents were upstairs getting ready to go out to dinner, and they were planning to drop me off here at the party. Matilda is definitely odd, but I kind of like odd people. We had a nice chat about World War II, which I'm writing a paper about, and she seemed to know a ton about it. She must read a lot of history. And she uses all these old expressions, like 'swell' and 'jeepers.' I thought that was sort of, well, charming. Then I told her I was going to the party and invited her along. She told me no thanks, and that I shouldn't go either. Almost as though . . ."

He trailed off, puzzled.

Kayla nodded impatiently, indicating that he should go on with the story.

"So when I told her I was just going to drop in for a little while, she gave me a stick of gum and insisted I chew it right then and there. It was the oddest thing. The gum was bright purple, but it didn't taste like grape or anything. It tasted pretty awful, frankly, but she watched while I chewed it a few times and then she let me go spit it out. Then she left. Bizarre, huh?"

Kayla thought rapidly. The gum must have been some sort of antidote, or preventive thing, that helped Tom unfreeze after drinking the punch. Because he *had* drunk the punch. He must have been frozen for a little while, until whatever it was Matilda had administered to him in the form of that gum had kicked in.

That settled it. Matilda had warned Tom not to come tonight. She knew something bad was going to happen. Could it be that the potion she had sold to Alice was supposed to do this—supposed to freeze everyone at the party? She must also know how to reverse it. Kayla had to find her right away. But even if she could find Matilda, how would Kayla be able to get all these frozen people to chew the antidote gum? And if they couldn't take the antidote, would they be frozen forever? She thought about her mom and her little brothers at home. She put the thought out of her mind. She had to move.

Kayla gestured to herself and pointed toward the

door, indicating that she was going to leave.

"Okay," said Tom. "But bundle up. It's snowing like crazy out there."

Kayla's boots were not where she'd left them in the kitchen. Of course. Mrs. Grafton had told Alice to put them into the front hall closet. She hurried out of the kitchen and down the hall, avoiding looking into the rooms with frozen people, and made her way to the closet. She opened it and shone the candle into the interior, only to find a mound of boots. She'd never find hers.

Luckily, she came up with a pair of warm, lined boots that looked about her size. She set down the candle and slipped her foot into one and then the other. They were a little big, but there was no time to search for another pair. She grabbed a warm parka—not hers—from a hanger and jammed a hat on her head.

By this time Tom had managed to hobble his way down the hall to join her. He picked a scarf up off the floor and helped her wrap it around herself, then thrust a pair of men's down gloves onto each of her hands. She waggled her oversize-gloved fingers in a good-bye wave. He opened the door for her. Outside, the snow was swirling, the wind gusting.

"Good luck," he said, his voice suddenly gentle.

She nodded grimly and was about to head out when he put his hand on her arm. She turned to him questioningly. He gave her a big hug. Then he shoved her outside.

As she stood on the front stoop, getting her bearings in the swirling snow, her mind roiled with conflicting emotions. It was so nice to be in Tom's arms, but she couldn't focus on that right now. She had to get to the shop . . . and it was not going to be easy.

There were at least ten inches of new snow on the ground already. The front steps had been clear before the party had started but were now heaped with snow. The walkway was as smooth as meringue, untouched by any footprints. It was deep, heavy snow, and it sucked at Kayla's too-large boots with every step, pulling them away from her heels as she walked. She put her head down and trudged down the front steps and down the driveway. It was a dark, howling night. She stepped as carefully as she could while still moving as quickly as possible. It wouldn't be good if she slipped and broke her arm. By the time she got to the sidewalk, the insides of the boots were filled with snow that had fallen in through the top, and Kayla's poor toes were starting to freeze.

Clouds covered the moon, and the streetlamps were out along Alice's block. It was so dark she could barely see her own feet as she walked. She prayed she wouldn't forget the way. Right turn at the corner. Two blocks down. Right turn onto the street where Esoterica was. She kept reciting the way to herself. It felt like miles.

She slipped and slid and once actually wiped out, getting snow up her sleeve and in her hair and feeling a sharp pain in her wrist as she tried to break her fall. But in her panicky state she barely noticed.

After what felt like hours, she finally turned onto the block where Matilda's store was. It was as dark as all the others. It seemed like the entire town had lost power. She broke into a run in her haste to get to the door, her scarf flying behind her, her hair whipping into her face beneath the hat she wore.

Esoterica was dark and quiet. No flashlights or candles shone from within. A CLOSED sign hung in the window. No footprints marred the snow. Clearly no one had gone in or out in quite some time. Her heart sank. Despair rose inside her. She started to cry, the wind freezing the tears on her face, silently sobbing with frustration, panic, and sheer terror. She tried not to think of her mother back in that horrible room, frozen, unseeing, not alive, not dead, but caught somewhere in between. She tried not to think about how she had felt ashamed of her mother's accent, and that maybe this whole thing was somehow her fault, a punishment for being ashamed. She vowed to herself that if she had the opportunity to feel her mother's arms around her again, she would never, ever be embarrassed by her mother's accent, or their old car, or about wearing her cousin's hand-me-downs. She was so lucky in so many ways. How could she not have realized it until now?

She tried the knob. Locked, of course. It seemed pointless to bang on the door, but she did so anyway. She waited, listening for a sound, anything. She heard nothing. She pounded again. She wiped away a circle of frost from the storefront window and tried to peer inside, but she could see nothing. No—wait. Had that been a flicker of movement?

She strained her eyes, trying to peer into the murky interior of the shop.

A pair of green eyes suddenly appeared in the swirl

of frost she'd cleared away. They stared out at her, unblinking.

She jumped back, startled, nearly stepping out of her boots. It was Jinx. He continued to stare at her, his eyes seeming to bore into her very soul.

And that was when the door flew open.

CHAPTER 14

Matilda stood in the doorway, regarding Kayla. It was impossible to read her expression in the darkness. She was motionless, her face in shadow, hands hanging limply at her sides. She was dressed in a sleeveless, shapeless cotton dress over a white ribbed turtleneck. On her feet she wore white socks shoved into an old pair of men's slippers. She didn't look like a twelve-year-old girl. Her outfit reminded Kayla of what her grandmother would wear around the house, with her hair coiled up in rollers, on a day when she planned to stay home and clean.

"What do *you* want?" Matilda finally asked.

Kayla pointed toward her own mouth and shook her head.

"Oh, I see. Were you foolish enough to take a sip of

punch? Must have spit it out, or you'd be much worse off than this."

Kayla stood there, her eyes pleading.

"All right, fine. You might as well come in. But just for a second. Don't expect me to entertain you with tea and crumpets."

Matilda stepped to the side, and Kayla slid past her and stepped into the shop.

It was dim inside, but Kayla was able to see much better than she'd expected. A dull red glow seemed to emanate from the walls, casting an eerie pink light on Matilda's skin. The two stood there, facing each other. Matilda crossed her arms and tilted her chin up, so that her bangs fell to the side and her owlish glasses glinted in the reddish gloom.

Kayla pulled off her snow-covered hat and shoved it into her pocket. She loosened the scarf around her neck. In the sudden heat of the shop, she felt faint and short of breath. She steadied herself on one of the counters, knocking over a small pyramid of bottles.

"So," said Matilda. "Since you can't speak, this will be a short conversation. After I went running over to that Tom Butler's house to give him a potion for his upset stomach, I discovered it was all a big joke. Someone had prank called me pretending to be Tom, and like an old fool, I fell for it. I've never been big on cell phones or any of that caller ID nonsense, so how was I to know it wasn't him?" She harrumphed. "Well, he was a nice enough chap, so I made him ingest a potion that would give him at least some immunity to the freeze-state, in case he was idiotic enough to go to the party after all."

Kayla looked around, hoping to find something to write with. She spied an old, spiral-bound notebook on one of the glass displays, with a pen next to it, and pounced on it. Then she scribbled a note on the inside front cover and shoved it across to Matilda.

> I'm so sorry. I was the one who prank called you. I know it was mean. I shouldn't have done it.

Matilda barely glanced at the note. Kayla wondered if she'd even read it.

"I'm not a total Luddite about technology," she said.

Kayla had no idea what a Luddite was, but she assumed it was something like a caveman.

"When I got back home, I called the operator, who told me how to do a reverse phone lookup. I saw that it was you who had called. A pity, really. I thought you were nicer than those others you associate with. I'd actually been thinking of calling *you* and telling you not to drink the punch. But I decided against it when I realized you were the one who'd played that mean trick on me. I figured you deserved whatever you got."

Kayla scribbled again.

Please, something went wrong with the love potion. It didn't work. It froze people instead

"Pah!" said Matilda, after glancing at what Kayla had written. "That was no love potion. It's a paralysis elixir. I've been working on the elixir for two years now, ever since Alice and her minions started taunting me back in fifth grade." She cackled. "Yes, I bided my time. The paralysis elixir was a complicated one. In addition to the usual difficult-to-find ingredients, I needed witchetty grubs all the way from Australia, some cytotoxin from a rattlesnake—you know it as snake venom—and some procaine hydrochloride."

Kayla raised her eyebrows as though to say, *What's that?*

"You know it as Novocain. Of course, no dentist is going to hand *that* over to a twelve-year-old, so I was forced to spray him with a perfume atomizer filled with sleeping spray at my last cleaning. Then I was able to clear out his drawer and walk out the front door, waving my new toothbrush to one and all."

Kayla shuddered. She wondered what the dentist must have thought when he came to.

"But I was missing the last ingredient—powdered African scarab beetles—until they practically landed in my lap. Imagine my pleasant surprise when I saw them in Talbert's terrarium. It was child's play to dose the janitor, borrow his passkey, and let myself into Talbert's classroom to collect the beetles. Once I had the paralysis solution complete, I had to wait for the perfect opportunity to enact my revenge. And then you walked right into the shop that day and made it all so easy for me. It was almost like fate played a role."

Her thin lips curled up into an evil smile as she watched Kayla pick up the pen.

Please, please can you give me back my voice?

"Why should I?" Matilda practically spat, after she read what Kayla had written. "You're as bad as the rest of them. You—"

Jinx chose that moment to leap up onto a display case next to Kayla. He sat down and curled his tail around his front paws, and then stared from Kayla to Matilda and back again to Kayla.

Matilda glared at the cat. Then she heaved a sigh. "Oh, all right, I get it, Jinx. I suppose she did bring you back here after you got hit, although I have my suspicions. She probably helped cause the accident in the first place. She probably let that wretched dog chase you into the street."

Kayla shook her head vigorously.

"Fine. Hold on a moment." Matilda turned and walked back through the velvet-curtained doorway. She seemed to be gone for a long time. Kayla tried to quell the panic that kept rising in her stomach. Outside, she could see the snow falling silently, heavily, covering her tracks, blanketing the quiet world. Anything could happen to her in here. She wondered what Tom was doing in that terrible house, surrounded by all the frozen people. She shuddered at the horror.

Matilda returned, holding something in her hand. She thrust her closed fist out to Kayla. Then she turned her hand over and opened it to reveal a small pillbox. She hit a button and it sprang open. "Take this. Suck on it. Your voice will be back in a few minutes."

Kayla shot her arm out, eager for the pill, but then hesitated. Matilda let out a low chuckle. "I'm afraid you don't have a choice, my dear," she said. "Either take this or lose your voice forever."

Kayla took the pale-orange, oval-shaped lozenge from Matilda's box and popped it into her mouth. It tasted bitter—terribly, awfully bitter. She gagged and retched. It tasted worse than anything she could imagine, worse than a spoonful of instant coffee, or sucking on the stems of a handful of dandelions. Her mouth twisted up, and she gagged again, trying not to throw up. But as she gagged, a small sound emerged from the back of her throat. As she swallowed, careful not to swallow the lozenge itself, she felt a sharp pain in her throat that reminded her of the time she'd had strep throat.

"I—can I—spit it out now?" Kayla rasped. She felt like she'd swallowed a handful of jagged glass.

"No. Suck the whole thing till it's gone," said Matilda

with a smug gleam in her eye. She seemed to enjoy watching Kayla's distress.

At last, Kayla felt she could talk without throwing up. "What's going to become of all those frozen people?" she gasped out.

Matilda raised an eyebrow. "All?"

"Yes," Kayla replied. "See, it's not just Alice, Pria, and Jess. Alice gave the punch to everyone at the party—even the parents. Everyone in that house is frozen, except for me . . . and well, Tom."

Matilda smiled slightly at the mention of Tom's name. "Nice boy," she murmured. "As for the others, it all depends on the dosage they took. I told that nasty friend of yours, Alice, to be very careful with the proportions, but did she listen? Doubtful. Anyway, the older you are, the more susceptible you tend to be. It works more quickly on older people. Still, pretty much everyone who drank the punch should be in an irreversible frozen state by the morning. Even I won't be able to help them. They won't be dead exactly. Just in a permanent state of vegetation. Their vital signs could continue indefinitely, but they'll never wake up."

Kayla's eyes welled up with tears. "My mom. My

mom is there, and she's frozen. She's all me and my brothers have."

"Then you'll be just like me, won't you?" said Matilda, her voice suddenly husky, almost quavering. "I don't have anyone. Now you'll see how it feels." She sniffed loudly.

Kayla felt her hysteria growing. She pulled out her phone. "I'll call the police," she said. "They'll come. They'll be able to help."

"There's nothing they'll be able to do," said Matilda. She stood up. "Now it's time for you to go."

CHAPTER 15

But Kayla couldn't move from fear. She thought about her mother, about her little brothers, about her classmates and her classmates' parents. She couldn't fail them. Everything now depended on her and her ability to reason with this strange, vindictive girl. She had to make Matilda understand just how much she would hurt so many people. She turned.

"Matilda, I'm sorry about your parents. I'm sorry that I made that prank call. You have every right to be angry with me. I know my friends weren't nice to you. You're right about them. They aren't true friends. They aren't even nice people, especially to anyone outside their clique. Sometimes they make *me* feel awful, so I can only imagine how they must make you feel. I understand what it feels like to be left out. Kids can be really mean."

Matilda shook back her bangs and glared at Kayla. "What do you know? You don't know the *half* of it," she spluttered. "You're as much to blame as the rest of them. Do you think I'm going to undo two years of work? I've plotted this revenge very carefully, and it worked perfectly! I'm sorry you got in the way, but what's done is done."

Matilda went on. "Sure, you're a nice enough person, but you're so worried about belonging, about fitting in, you let them push you around. You let them talk you into doing things you shouldn't do. You're *smart*, too. I see your name on the honor roll every semester. You should appreciate what you have." She put out a hand to stroke Jinx. He let her pet his back once, twice, and then he jumped off the counter and trotted over to where Kayla was standing near the door. He wove himself around in a figure eight between her feet, purring loudly.

Matilda stared at the cat. "All right, all right! I get it!" Then she raised her head and looked at Kayla. "Come. Sit." She pointed toward two chairs that were arranged side by side in the shadowy back corner of the shop.

They had matching worn-out red upholstery with gold-painted wooden trim. They looked as though they had once been very fancy chairs.

Despite her panic, and her feeling that time was running out fast, Kayla did as she was told. She knew the only way to help her mother and the others was if she could win over Matilda.

Matilda sat, looking lost in thought, as though debating what she wanted to say. Finally she leaned in to whisper something to Kayla. "I am not what I seem," she confessed.

Kayla nodded. She didn't dare distract Matilda with questions.

"I don't just work at this store. I own it. There is no 'owner,' other than me."

Kayla raised her eyebrows, but still said nothing.

"I was once a mean girl. Just like your friend Alice. I was pretty and spoiled, and the boys all flocked around me like hogs to slop. I loved being the center of attention. I loved how other girls tried to look like me, to dress like me. But that was seventy-five years ago."

"Seventy-five—"

"Yes. Close your mouth," Matilda snapped.

"Seventy-five years ago, when I was twelve years old. I may still look as though I'm twelve, but I am, in fact, an old lady of eighty-seven. Heaven knows I have all the ailments of old age—bad eyesight, sore feet, aching hips. Seventy-five years ago, I was given a potion without my knowledge, a potion that caused me to appear to never age. I had been haughty and cruel and horrid to a girl at my school day in and day out. She was a mousy little thing, so easy to torment. My friends and I tortured her with our sarcasm, our teasing, our tricks. The teachers never had any idea. Well, I chose the wrong person to pick on. She was smart. If she'd been born today, she'd have been a Nobel Prize–winning chemist. But back then, girls didn't think that way. They didn't dream of careers in science."

She shook her head and looked out the window, lost in thought. Kayla resisted the impulse to leap from her chair, to scream, *Get on with it!* She sat and waited for Matilda to continue.

"Unbeknownst to me, this girl had taught herself how to make potions. Strong potions. It was *she* who did this to me, who gave me an antiaging elixir. She laced some chocolates with it and left me a box of them for

Valentine's Day, with a note that said the gift was from 'a secret admirer.' One piece of chocolate was all it took. I never grew up. I never got to live my life."

"I'm sorry, Matilda," whispered Kayla. And she meant it.

Matilda's jaw tightened. "When I figured out what had happened to me, I vowed to learn the craft as well. I was smart too! My parents removed me from school when they realized something was wrong with my development, and they hired a tutor to teach me. They were embarrassed by me."

"What became of the girl?" asked Kayla.

"Died," said Matilda flatly. "She fell from a window, although to this day I wonder if it was an accident, or if she took her own life. After all, I had made her so miserable with my bullying, and then she must have felt some guilt for what she did to me." Matilda pulled a large handkerchief from her pocket and blew her nose loudly. "From that day on, I vowed to stop all the mean girls I encountered. That's why I froze your friend Alice, along with her awful friends."

"Matilda," said Kayla gently, "I am so sorry for what you have suffered. But surely you don't want to do harm to so many people, people who never did you any wrong. And even Alice—do you really want to wipe out so many lives? My own mother works so hard. She's a single mom with four kids. Think about who she'd be leaving behind. I have a little brother named Timothy. He's only seven, but you should see what a great little hockey player he is. He has curly brown hair and—" Kayla began to sob.

Matilda sighed, and Kayla looked up. The other girl's expression had softened ever so slightly. "You're right. I can't go through with it," she said solemnly. "I may be a bitter old fool, but I can't actually do this. I guess I really didn't think of all the other people I'd hurt, only those nasty girls. I'll give you a vaporous compound that will reverse the paralysis condition. Wait here."

She stood up and went into the back room. Kayla wiped her eyes, leaned back, and breathed.

"Take this," said Matilda, upon returning. She handed Kayla a thick black candle. "Burning it will release the antidote fumes into the air. As soon as the frozen people inhale it, they'll begin to revive. It may take fifteen or twenty minutes for a full recovery—assuming they haven't ingested too much of the potion and its effects can still be reversed. There's certainly that danger."

Kayla leaped out of the chair, clutching the candle to her chest. Then she stuck it into her jacket pocket and zipped it securely. "Thank you, Matilda," she said. "Thank you. You've just done a merciful thing."

Matilda opened the door for Kayla. "I'd advise you to hurry," she said matter-of-factly.

CHAPTER 16

Kayla flung herself back out into the whirling, windy snow and took off running. By clenching her toes inside her boots, she managed to keep them from slipping off her feet, and the thick layer of snow gave her more traction now than when she'd come the other way. Her own footprints from half an hour before were the only ones visible on the sidewalk, and the snow was so heavy, they were already nearly filled in.

Her fear, panic, and determination to get back as quickly as humanly possible were so strong that it seemed only a few seconds had passed before she caught sight of Alice's house, looming dark and gray against the black night sky. With a sudden burst of adrenaline, she broke into a flat-out sprint up the driveway. One of her boots slipped off her foot entirely, but she barely noticed, covering the last twenty yards with one of her feet completely bare. She didn't feel the cold until she'd flung open the door and stepped inside.

Tom was there at the door when she burst in, and he helped her pull off her coat. She stomped her one boot and bent her other leg up so that she could brush away the worst of the snow clinging to her icy-cold foot.

"No change," he said. "No one has moved, and there's still no phone service. What did you find out?"

He had a pad and pen ready for her, but she pushed them away. "I can talk," she said. "I'll explain how I got my voice back later. But I have a way to reverse their condition. We have to burn this candle. There's no time to lose. Can you help me find some matches?"

The two might have been a comical sight under other circumstances, Kayla with one booted foot and one bare one, Tom with one bandaged ankle, hopping mostly on his good foot, opening drawers and lifting lids on decorative pots. As they searched, Kayla explained to Tom that the candle smoke would reverse the effects of the punch, or so she hoped.

"Got some!" yelled Kayla, who was over by the

fireplace. She'd found some long matches in a cardboard cylinder, meant to light fires in a fireplace. She struck a match and held it to the wick. The black candle flashed and sputtered, like a Fourth of July sparkler, and then turned into a deep purple flame. Purple smoke rose from the flame in curling tendrils, almost as though it had a will of its own.

"Oh, *man!*" said Tom, coughing and scrunching his nose. "That smells *awful!*"

It did. It smelled acrid and sulfurous and reminded Kayla of a musty old kitchen sponge, her baby cousin's diaper pail, and a pot of soup she had once forgotten about and had left on a burner until it blackened and smoked.

"You can move faster than I can," said Tom. "You take charge of the candle. I'll go dump out the punch bowls."

Although the room was dark and it was difficult to see, Kayla noticed that the purple smoke didn't seem to dissipate the way an ordinary candle's might; it twirled and coiled, remaining suspended in rings and curlicues around the room. Choking and half gagging at the smell, she first carried the candle into the area with the coats, where her mother was still sitting, halfway through pulling on her boots.

Kayla wafted the candle as close as she could beneath her mother's nostrils, taking care not to get it close to her hair, and watched and waited anxiously.

Some of the smoke seemed to reach her mother's nose, as though her mother was inhaling it. Kayla's every instinct told her to wait and watch her mother, but she knew there were a lot of people's parents who needed her help, and timing could be critical. She hurried into the other room, the candle at arm's length, trailing purple fumes as she moved around the frozen people.

Tom, meanwhile, had picked up the punch bowl. He held it cradled to his chest and looked toward the kitchen, and then toward the front door. "I'm not going to be able to step over that dude," he called to Kayla, gesturing toward the man she had knocked over, who was lying across the doorway to the pantry. "Front door's closer."

As Kayla continued wafting the candle smoke beneath the nostrils of the frozen parents, she watched Tom hobble awkwardly toward the front door, sloshing himself with the punch. He opened the door, looked outside, and shrugged. Then he pitched the entire bowl outside. Even from the other room, Kayla could hear a dull thud and then the crack of the bowl.

"Oops," said Tom with a shrug.

"I need to check on my mom," said Kayla, hurrying back to the room with the coats.

Her mother was beginning to stir. Her eyes were now closed, and rather than leaning forward, she was starting to sink backward, ever so slowly, against the coats draped over the back of the couch. Her head began to move from side to side, and a low moan escaped her lips.

"Kay, she's going to be all right," said Tom gently but urgently. "We need to get downstairs right away."

Kayla nodded and led the way toward the basement. She stepped gingerly over the fallen man, who was slowly beginning to stir, then turned and helped Tom hobble over him as well. Then they made their way through the pantry, into the kitchen, and down the basement stairs.

CHAPTER 17

The power went back on before they'd gotten to the bottom of the stairs. With eerie suddenness, the music resumed playing. The movie, which they could see through the far doorway, started back up, and the strings of red, heart-shaped lanterns lit up the room in a rosy glow. The frozen kids looked all the more eerie in the sudden festive party atmosphere.

Kayla hurried down the remaining stairs, holding the candle out in front of her, cupping the flame so it wouldn't blow out. She moved from kid to kid and tried to waft the smoke with her free hand so that it floated beneath each kid's nostrils. The sulfurous smell grew even worse down in the basement, where the rooms were less well ventilated and the ceilings lower. It was easier to see the purple fog now, coiling and twining and then slowly wafting upward, forming a smelly purple cloud near the ceiling.

Tom hobbled over to the table with the punch bowl on it, picked it up, and half walked, half hopped toward the door to the laundry room, where Kayla had told him he would find a sink. He left a trail of red punch on the carpet behind him.

As she continued to move around the room, wafting the candle's fumes under people's noses, she heard a loud splash, and then a thump and the shattering of the other bowl.

"Uh-oh!" she heard Tom's muffled voice say.

Soon he had rejoined her in the main room. They stood, staring from person to person, searching for a sign of movement, the flutter of an eye. But there was nothing. The kids all remained frozen.

"Are we too late?" wailed Kayla, clutching Tom's arm and looking at him wild-eyed. Smoke continued to pour off the candle.

Tom looked grim. "Keep waiting. It's got to happen. The grown-ups took a while. Maybe kids take even longer." But he didn't sound sure.

They stood, watching, waiting, listening to the music change from one upbeat dance song to another.

And then Kayla heard a cough.

"What is that *smell*?" said someone across the room.

"Gross!" said another.

Kayla's eyes were on Alice. As though someone had unpaused a DVD, Alice suddenly began moving again, running her hands through her hair, continuing her movement from earlier. Then her head snapped to attention, and she looked around. "Yuck! Ick! Did someone try to flush, like, their *coat* down the toilet or something?"

She crossed the room, looking like she was planning to go upstairs to find her mother, when she skidded to a stop in front of Kayla and Tom. She stared at the smoke that was pouring and swirling from the candle. Her hand flew to her nose.

"It's that *candle*!" she cried, half-disbelieving, half-furious.

Kayla had forgotten that she was still holding the burning black candle. Hastily she blew it out.

By now all the kids appeared to be unfrozen, moving around, and seemingly fine. Nearly everyone was coughing, sputtering, and saying, "Eeeeeew!"

"Oh, sorry about the candle, Alice," said Kayla, smiling weakly. "I can explain, but you might not want me to right this second. It's about—"

"What's that you've got all down your shirt?" Alice demanded of Tom, pointing. "Are you an *ax* murderer or something?"

He glanced down at the front of his yellow sweater. It was soaked in red punch. He looked back up and grinned sheepishly. "Punch?" he said.

Alice looked around the room slowly. Then she turned back to Kayla and Tom. "What did you do to the punch? It's not there!"

Pria and Jess emerged from the other room. They came and stood on either side of Alice and crossed their arms.

"I know where the punch is," said Pria.

"Me too," said Jess.

"They dumped it out," said Pria.

"It's sloshed all over the laundry sink," said Jess.

"And the bowl is broken," said Pria.

"Yeah, sorry about the bowl," said Tom. "It kind of slipped out of my hands. I was trying to dump it out while standing on one foot." He pointed apologetically down at his sprained ankle.

"Alice, we can explain," said Kayla.

"I know just what you were up to," Alice said to her in a steely voice. "You told him to dump it out because you saw him talking to me and you were jealous. You knew what would happen, didn't you? And you couldn't deal with *your* crush crushing on someone *else*, namely me!"

"No, it's not like that," said Kayla quickly.

She felt Tom turn to look at her. She couldn't meet his eye, but she could tell he was grinning, no doubt psyched about being called her crush.

"I've had it up to here with you, Kayla," said Alice.

Jess and Pria nodded vigorously in agreement. "So have we!" they said, nearly at the same time.

Then Alice noticed Kayla's feet. "You're wearing my boot!" she said. "Where's the other one?"

"Oh. Right. The boots." Suddenly Kayla realized that the boots she'd taken from the front closet had been Alice's. She'd been with her when she'd bought them! "I think the other one is . . . outside somewhere."

Alice's mouth fell open. She leaned toward Kayla, her eyes narrowed with fury. She looked like she was about to bellow at the top of her lungs. But then she appeared to think better of it. She looked around the room at the kids, who had resumed what they had been doing before they'd been frozen, as if nothing had happened. They were dancing, eating, and drinking. One boy was standing on a chair, trying to fan the last of the foul-smelling fumes out of an open window. Kayla knew Alice would do anything not to cause a scene, not to disrupt her party.

"That is just beyond belief," said Alice in a low voice. "I know you wish you were me. I know you don't have nice clothes and you wish you had my stuff, Kayla. I was so nice to you. I let you into my group."

Pria and Jess nodded.

"We let you sit with us in the cafeteria," Pria chimed in.

"We put up with your geeky studying," added Jess.

"And your ugly clothes," said Pria.

"And your *refusal* to do anything about your hair," said Alice. "And then how do you repay me? By *stealing* from me! Taking my *boots* without permission and then *losing* one is—"

"I didn't steal them!" said Kayla.

Alice kept going. "And let's not even get started on

your mother. I mean, honestly. Aren't you embarrassed to be seen pulling into places in that sloppy jalopy she drives, with a backseat full of bratty little brothers? And please. That accent?"

"You leave my mother out of this," said Kayla in a tone cold as ice.

Alice blinked, surprised.

Kayla flashed with anger. After the horrors she'd suffered that evening, the fears and anxieties, the dreadful race through the storm, the pleading on their behalf . . . she wasn't going to stand for Alice's attitude one minute longer.

"Listen, Alice," she said in a loud, clear voice. "And you listen too, Jess and Pria. It's time you learned that you are not the center of the universe. Your mean behavior has terrible consequences, consequences beyond anything you can imagine. Your hateful words to other people don't just hurt others, although they certainly do, but they can cause terrible consequences to you, too!"

Alice flipped her hair and rolled her eyes.

"And here's a news flash: There's more to life than shopping and getting your hair highlighted and your nails done. Just for the record, I *like* my mom's car. We've had it my whole life. I *like* my mom's accent. I *like* my bratty little brothers. And I *like* my hair. And my mom has better things to spend money on than tons of clothes I don't need. Maybe you should spend a little less time worrying about your appearance and a little more time thinking about others around you. Your lives are going to be pretty empty if you keep acting this way."

Pria grimaced.

Jess looked like she might burst into tears.

Alice was speechless.

"Alice, I'm sorry about the punch bowl," said Kayla. "We didn't mean to break it. I told you we had a good reason to do it, and I'll explain later, when we're not in a room full of people."

"Oh, no you won't," said Alice, who seemed to have recovered from the shock of Kayla's words. "I think you should leave now. And take your little boyfriend with you."

"Hey, I'm not *that* little," said Tom lightheartedly. "My feet are size eleven already, so the doctor says I'm going to be tall."

Alice, Pria, and Jess wheeled on Tom, eyes flashing.

"Just pointing that out," he concluded.

Suddenly Alice's mother came clattering down the basement steps. Because of her high, wobbly heels, she was obliged to walk down sideways. "Alice!" she said, swaying slightly and catching her balance. "*What* happened to the punch bowl? Someone took it off the table and threw it outside, right down the front steps, and *shattered* it! That was expensive pottery! Do you *know* how much I *paid* for that bowl?"

Alice turned back to Kayla and Tom. She put her hands on her hips.

Alice and Kayla exchanged a look.

"I'll tell you later, Mother," said Alice, and her tone was cold and steely. "Just *forget* about the dumb punch bowl for now. This will not ruin my party, okay? But Kayla and Tom here were just leaving."

Mrs. Grafton seemed to recover her manners. She smiled a thin, insincere smile and said brightly, "Well, I hope you two had a nice time. I had a lovely time talking to your mother, Katie. She was very informative about the admissions process at the academy. I look forward to spending more time with her! And I just adore her charming accent!"

"Thanks for a fun party, Mrs. Grafton," said Kayla.

She and Tom slipped past her and made their way up the basement stairs, Tom clumping up on his crutch.

Kayla's mother was standing in the kitchen, wearing her coat and boots, her hand on the door to the outside.

"Mom!" yelled Kayla, bounding across the kitchen and throwing herself into her mother's arms. "I'm so glad to see you!"

Her mother reared back in surprise, but she hugged Kayla back. "I'm so glad you're glad," she said.

"Can we go home with you now?"

"Oh!" said her mother. "I thought you were planning to sleep over. Is everything all right?"

"Everything's great. Better than great. But I think I've had enough sleepovers for a while. This is Tom Butler from my science class," said Kayla, releasing her mother from the hug and gesturing to Tom. "Can we drop him off at his home?"

"Of course," said her mother.

"I'll just run and find my boots and my coat and stuff and be right back," said Kayla. She hurried into the front hall, took off Alice's one boot, and placed it carefully inside the closet. *No doubt they will find the other boot tomorrow,* she thought. *Or maybe in the spring, when the snow finally melts.* With the lights back on, she found her coat and boots right away, and her bag and her flat black shoes, too. She shoved them into her bag and was back in the kitchen just moments later.

The grown-up party seemed to have drawn breath again, and Kayla was happy to see everyone talking, milling around, and looking normal once more. The tall man she'd knocked over was standing next to a platter of mini pigs-in-a-blanket, shoveling them into his mouth as though he hadn't eaten all day. She spotted Alice's father standing next to a potted plant, having a heated conversation with someone on his phone.

Quietly she closed the door and left.

EPILOGUE

FIVE YEARS LATER

"Wow, I haven't been back to this neighborhood in ages," said Kayla, clutching Tom's arm tightly to her side as they walked down a charming little block in Fairbridge. It was a beautiful spring day. Tulips swayed in the gentle breeze in front of a modern-looking coffee bar, which took up most of the block. Across the street were several trendy clothing boutiques.

Tom stopped and looked down at her. "Kay, you do know where we are, right? It's the same block where that store used to be. The one that Matilda used to own."

Kayla's jaw dropped. "You're right. I haven't been back to this part of town since my mom became head of admissions at the academy and they gave us an on-campus house to live in. This coffee shop used to be an antique store, and a dress store. I wonder what ever happened to Matilda? She disappeared after that Valentine's Day."

They were both quiet, staring at the place where Esoterica had once been, lost in their own thoughts. They'd talked a lot about the events of that fateful night five years ago. After that night, Alice, Jess, and Pria had basically stopped talking to Kayla. For a while she'd sat by herself in the cafeteria, miserable and lonely, but eventually she'd made friends with a new group of kids, through Tom, and had discovered they were pretty cool in their own way. The next year she and Tom had both been accepted at Fairbridge Academy on full scholarships. They had gone out briefly and remained friends. And this past summer, they had rediscovered each other, beyond being "just friends."

"Hey, we're second-semester seniors, and we both got into the same college," said Tom. "I think we deserve to take the afternoon off from studying, don't you? Let's chill a little, for a change. I'll buy you a latte."

Kayla smiled. "Sounds good to me."

The coffee shop was warm and inviting and smelled

heavenly, like roast coffee and baking muffins. They found a table near the window and sat across from each other, holding hands.

"Have you seen those girls around much?" he asked.

Kayla knew who he meant. She shook her head. "No, I think Pria and Jess are still at Fairbridge High School. I heard Pria became pretty good at gymnastics. And Jess was into diving. But we lost touch after middle school, after I came to the academy. I saw them a couple of years ago at the mall—they looked just the same as ever, but they pretended they didn't know me."

"Yeah, I kind of fell out of that group of guys I used to hang out with, after my cousin Scott moved to Arizona," said Tom. "I think he was the only reason they tolerated having me around. It was satisfying to grow to be six-three, though. I'm petty enough to admit, it was pretty cool to score twenty-eight points against Fairbridge High's basketball team this past season, especially with Nick Maroulis trying to guard me."

Kayla rolled her eyes. "Honestly, Tom. I don't know what I see in you."

"Yes, you do," he said, squeezing both her hands in his and grinning at her with that half smile she had always loved so much. He reached across the table and lovingly tucked a strand of hair behind her ear.

"I heard that Alice's parents sent her away, to some boarding school in Switzerland, I think," Kayla continued. "I haven't laid eyes on her since eighth grade. Maybe she grew up a little bit. I hope so."

The waitress appeared at their table, holding two steaming cups, which she set down in front of them.

"What are these?" asked Tom, puzzled. "We haven't ordered yet."

The waitress smiled. "Two double tall, triple-vanilla, extra-caramel macchiatos, extra hot, with whipped," she said. "Compliments of an old friend."

Tom and Kayla exchanged surprised looks, then turned and looked around the coffee shop. The waitress left.

"Do you know anyone in here?" Kayla asked Tom.

"Not a one," he replied.

"They sure smell delicious," said Kayla, closing her eyes and breathing in the fragrant aroma of her drink.

They both lifted their cups to their lips.

Tom spat his back out. "Don't drink it!" he hissed.

Kayla spat the sip she'd just taken back into her cup and looked at him. "What's the matter?"

"Does that girl over there look familiar to you?"

Tom was gesturing toward the corner of the room, directly behind Kayla. She turned around in her chair.

A girl was sitting by herself at a table. She looked about twelve. Kayla whipped back around and stared at Tom.

"Is that . . . Alice?"

He nodded. "Sure looks like it."

"But—but—how *could* it be? The girl over there looks like she's only twelve or thirteen years old!"

"I know. Like she hasn't grown a day since that night."

Kayla's eyes grew huge. "You don't think . . . did Matilda . . . oh no."

Tom picked up where she'd left off. "Matilda must have given Alice the same potion she'd been given. The one that stopped her from growing up."

Kayla was racking her brain, trying to remember. "It must have been those green mints she gave the three of them that day. Matilda told us they were for our complexions and our hair. I remember I wanted to take one, but she wouldn't let me have one. She told me I was a hopeless case."

"She was protecting you from their fate."

"Now that I think about it, that time I saw Pria and

Jess at the mall? They didn't look like they'd aged either." Kayla passed a hand over her brow, horror written across her face.

"Don't look. She's standing up. She's walking out."

Kayla stared straight ahead. Tom looked down at his drink. The girl passed their table without a glance at them. As she pushed her way through the door, Kayla darted a look at her.

The girl was looking back at Kayla. It was definitely Alice. She was still beautiful, with her lovely, glossy hair. But her face had changed and hardened. A sinister smile played on her lips. She pulled the door closed behind her and hurried away.

"Did you swallow any of it?" asked Tom hoarsely.

"No, I don't think so," said Kayla. "I might have had some foam on my lip, though. I might have tasted a bit of that." She looked at Tom, wild-eyed. "Do you think she did something to our drinks?"

Tom shrugged. "I don't know, Kay. I guess we'll have to wait and find out."

DO NOT FEAR—
WE HAVE ANOTHER CREEPY TALE FOR YOU!

TURN THE PAGE FOR A SNEAK PEEK AT

You're invited to a

CREEPOVER™

What a Doll!

One Friday night Lizzy Draper and Emmy Spencer were watching TV and eating popcorn at Lizzy's house. This was because Lizzy didn't seem to want to do anything else.

"Pass the popcorn, Lizzy?" Emmy asked her best friend.

Lizzy passed it over with a slightly annoyed look. "It's Liz, remember?" she asked Emmy. "Now that I'm not five anymore?"

"Oh, right. Sorry, Liz," Emmy mumbled. Emmy had a bad feeling in her stomach, the same feeling she'd been having for a few months now. Things were different between the lifelong best friends. There was no denying it. It was simple: Now that they were in seventh grade,

Lizzy had become popular and Emmy had not. Lizzy was talking to boys, and Emmy was not. Lizzy was wearing lip gloss, and Emmy was not. Lizzy—

"Hey, you know something?" Lizzy interrupted Emmy's thoughts. "You could maybe start going by a more mature name yourself."

"What do you mean? Change my name?" Emmy asked.

"No, silly," Lizzy said. "Just go by something like Em. Or Emma."

"Em might be okay," Emmy responded. "But my full name's not Emma. It's Emily."

"Right, but Emma is much cooler," Lizzy said, looking totally serious.

"I kind of like Em," said Emmy. "But it would take some getting used to. Hey, I know. Instead of Liz, I could call you Lizard." Emmy laughed at her own joke.

"Like when I was three?" Lizzy asked sarcastically.

Emmy thought it might be a good idea to change the subject. "So what are we going to be for the costume party this year?"

Lizzy paused and examined the pattern on the rug. "Oh," she said. "I was going to tell you. I'm going to do a group costume with Cadence and Sophie."

Ouch. Emmy tried to keep the hurt out of her voice. "But we had so much fun last year," she said.

The costume party was part of their school's spirit week, which was only a few weeks away. When Lizzy and Emmy were in sixth grade, they heard rumors about how competitive some of the kids got with their costumes, and they were a little scared to participate. But then Emmy had the most brilliant idea: Lizzy could dress up as a bug and Emmy could go as a can of bug spray. Lizzy had loved it and so had everyone else. They even won an honorable mention for such a creative costume—an honor very few sixth graders ever received.

Emmy had been thinking of ideas for this year's costume for months now, but apparently it was all for nothing. At this moment, Emmy was feeling a lot like she was an actual bug and Lizzy was the spray.

"I know," Lizzy said. "Sorry."

Lizzy's mom, Marilyn, poked her head into the family room. "You girls should turn off the TV soon," she said.

"There's nothing else to do, Mom," Lizzy said with a hint of a whine. Emmy couldn't help but notice that

Lizzy had stopped calling her mother "Mommy," which Emmy still called her mother. What was with all these name changes?

"I can't believe my ears," her mom said. "You two have always found fun things to do together at your sleepovers." It was true. They'd make crazy concoctions in the kitchen, pretend to open up a beauty parlor, write short plays and perform them for their parents, carve bars of soap into funny shapes, and do plenty of other creative stuff.

Lizzy sighed loudly and said nothing more, finally turning off the television when it was time for dinner. The two girls sat silently at the table they had sat at together so many times before, since they were babies in high chairs. Their moms had met when they were pregnant, and because they were next-door neighbors on a street deep in the heart of Brooklyn, New York, they'd spent countless hours with their baby girls in their kitchens, out running errands, at the playground, and even on family vacations together. Lizzy and Emmy had always been inseparable, just like their moms. Until lately.

Twirling spaghetti on her fork, Emmy was lost in thought. How could she feel so lonely with her best friend beside her? Maybe it was because they weren't really best friends anymore. That thought made her so sad she had to put her fork down. It was all she could do to keep herself from putting her head down on the table.

"What's the matter, Emmy?" Marilyn asked.

"Nothing," Emmy said. There was a time when she could tell Marilyn anything, and this wasn't that time. Marilyn and Joanne, Emmy's mom, had always depended on each other to take care of the other's daughter in a pinch. If Joanne couldn't get away from work and Emmy was sick at school, Marilyn would pick her up at the nurse's office. If Marilyn had to go to a meeting out of town, Joanne would watch Lizzy until she got back. It was like each girl had two moms. Of course, it was even better than that because it was also like each girl had a sister— Lizzy was an only child, and Emmy had a little brother.

Living next door to each other had always been so much fun. The best part of all was that they could see right into each other's bedrooms. They had all sorts of fun with this, shining laser lights or flashlights on each other's walls in the dark and throwing things back and forth through their open windows. They did have one rule they agreed upon long ago, though: no spying.

As the girls cleared the dishes, Emmy noticed Lizzy looking at her closely. She seemed to be focused on Emmy's long dark hair, which she wore in two braids. On the way up the stairs to Lizzy's room, Lizzy swished one of Emmy's braids like a horse's tail.

"I have a great idea," Lizzy said as they entered her room. "Let's give you a makeover."

Emmy was pleased that Lizzy wanted to do something, *anything*, with her. And they had played with makeup before. They used to love playing dress-up and putting on fashion shows for their parents. It would be fun. *This sleepover isn't going to be totally awful after all*, Emmy thought.

"Awesome," Emmy said, smiling. "Where's your mom's makeup case?" It was what they'd always used when they played dress-up.

"No makeup," Lizzy announced, swishing Emmy's other braid. "Hair."

"Oh. Okay," Emmy said, and removed the rubber band from each braid. She ran her fingers through each braid to undo it, splaying out her long pretty hair over her shoulders. Her hair was so long it almost reached her butt.

Lizzy looked at Emmy's hair thoughtfully. "I have

a vision," she said, grinning, and left the room. "I'll be right back."

Emmy sat cross-legged on the floor, facing the mirror. She couldn't wait to see what Lizzy was going to do. Would she weave a sophisticated inside-out French braid, like she did so well? Use a curling iron? She was so relieved that Lizzy seemed more like her old self that she didn't notice what Lizzy was holding in her hand when she came back into the room.

Scissors.

Lizzy help them up like a magician's wand. "You're going to look great, Em," she promised.

Emmy's heart stopped. "Um, Liz . . . ," she stammered. "I don't want an actual haircut. I thought you were just going to braid it or something."

"But haven't you noticed how badly you need one?" Lizzy asked. "We're in seventh grade now, but your hair is stuck in fourth."

Emmy instinctively put her hands to her hair to protect it. What would her mother say if she came home with her hair cut off? She loved her daughter's long hair. So did Emmy, actually. She loved feeling it cover her back, she loved brushing it, she loved braiding it herself. She'd never wanted shorter hair. For her entire life Emmy had never allowed it to be cut more than an inch to get rid of split ends. It had always been long. And so had Lizzy's light blond hair until this year, when she'd gone for a shoulder-length cut that she described as "sassier than long hair."

Emmy was still stammering. "Plenty of grown-ups have long hair," she pointed out.

Lizzy frowned. "Oh, never mind," she said. "You're hopeless."

"I'm sorry," Emmy said, making sure her voice didn't crack. She was on the verge of tears. Things had been going so much better in the last few minutes, and now Lizzy was disappointed. She was giving up on Emmy.

"Whatever," Lizzy said like she really didn't care. "I was just trying to help you. Forget it. Let's just go watch TV again."

Emmy's heart sank deeper into her stomach. Her mind raced. Was there some way to salvage this sleepover? Yes, there was.

"How about if you just trim it?" Emmy asked. "I don't mind having it cut a little bit. It might be . . . cool," she added.

Lizzy smiled. "Excellent," she said. "It *will* be cool. I promise. First let me wash it in the sink, like at a real hair salon."

They went into the bathroom, where Lizzy gently sudsed up Emmy's hair and carefully rinsed it. Then she even added conditioner. Emmy loved the feeling of Lizzy's hands massaging her scalp. Lizzy was right. It was just like being at the salon. All the while, Lizzy was humming happily. It was just like old times. She helped Emmy stand up, wrapped one towel around her head and one around her shoulders, and led her back into her bedroom, where she combed out her hair and turned Emmy away from the mirror. Emmy felt like she was at a fancy spa.

"Here, sit on this towel," Lizzy said, "so we don't get hair all over the floor." Emmy moved onto the towel.

Just as Lizzy started cutting, her cell phone rang. She put down the scissors and grabbed the phone.

"Hey, Cadence!" she said happily. "What's up? No, I'm not doing anything."

Yes you are, Emmy thought sadly.

But Lizzy continued the conversation for a few more minutes before hanging up. Then she continued cutting.

Emmy was faced away from the mirror, but it felt to her like Lizzy was cutting off quite a lot.

"I think you're cutting too much," she said to Lizzy. "Let me just see in the mirror."

Lizzy put the scissors down and put her hands on her hips. "Do you trust me or not?" she said.

"I trust you," Emmy lied.

Lizzy continued snipping away, stopping twice to check text messages, which she smiled at but did not say anything about.

More snipping. A lot more snipping, actually.

"Okay, you can look now," Lizzy said proudly. And for the next few moments, everything went in slow motion for Emmy.

She turned around and looked at her reflection. At first she wasn't sure if she was hallucinating, but then she snapped back to reality. And what she saw in the mirror made her scream.

WANT MORE CREEPINESS?

Then you're in luck, because P. J. Night has some more scares for you and your friends!

One Potion, Many Possibilities

How many words of three letters or more can you make from the letters in the words LOVE POTIONS? Compete against yourself or your friends. Make sure you have enough paper on hand. There are lots and lots of possibilities!

YOU'RE INVITED TO . . .
CREATE YOUR OWN SCARY STORY!

Do you want to turn your sleepover into a creepover? Telling a spooky story is a great way to set the mood. P. J. Night has written a few sentences to get you started. Fill in the rest of the story and have fun scaring your friends.

You can also collaborate with your friends on this story by taking turns. Have everyone at your sleepover sit in a circle. Pick one person to start. She will add a sentence or two to the story, cover what she wrote with a piece of paper, leaving only the last word or phrase visible, and then pass the story to the next girl. Once everyone has taken a turn, read the scary story you created together aloud!

Brrrrring! trilled the bell on the door as I let myself into the curiosity shop. "Hello," I called out, but was met with silence. Funny, I could have sworn I saw someone staring out the window a minute ago. I walked farther into the shop, eyeing the mysteriously labeled bottles and carefully sidestepping the grotesque sculptures that lined the floor. A grimacing gargoyle statue sat perched on a shelf to my right. Was I imagining things or was it following me with its gaze? Then something caught my eye—an ornate bottle inside a dusty display case. I leaned over the glass to get a closer look, when all of a sudden . . .

_____

_____

_____

_____

_____

_____

_____

THE END

THE END

A lifelong night owl, **P. J. NIGHT** often works furiously into the wee hours of the morning, writing down spooky tales and dreaming up new stories of the supernatural and otherworldly. Although P. J.'s whereabouts are unknown at this time, we suspect the author lives in a drafty, old mansion where the floorboards creak when no one is there and the flickering candlelight creates shadows that creep along the walls. We truly wish we could tell you more, but we've been sworn to keep P. J.'s identity a secret . . . and it's a secret we will take to our graves!